JUST PERVS

JUST PERVS

JESS TAYLOR

Book*hug Press

Toronto, 2019

FIRST EDITION

The production of this book was made possible through the generous assistance of the Canada Council for the Arts and the Ontario Arts Council. Book*hug Press also acknowledges the support of the Government of Canada through the Canada Book Fund and the Government of Ontario through the Ontario Book Publishing Tax Credit and the Ontario Book Fund.

ONTARIO ARTS COUNCIL
CONSEIL DES ARTS DE L'ONTARIO
an Ontario government agency
un organisme du gouvernement de l'Ontario

Book*hug Press acknowledges the land on which it operates. For thousands of years it has been the traditional land of the Huron-Wendat, the Seneca, and most recently, the Mississaugas of the Credit River. Today, this meeting place is still the home to many Indigenous people from across Turtle Island, and we are grateful to have the opportunity to work on this land.

Library and Archives Canada Cataloguing in Publication

Title: Just pervs / Jess Taylor.
Names: Taylor, Jess, 1989- author.
Description: First edition. | Short stories.
Identifiers: Canadiana (print) 20190147075 | Canadiana (ebook) 20190147083
ISBN 9781771665148 (softcover) | ISBN 9781771665155 (HTML)
ISBN 9781771665162 (PDF) | ISBN 9781771665179 (Kindle)
Classification: LCC PS8639.A9519 J88 2019 | DDC C813/.6—dc23

Printed in Canada

For my friends

CONTENTS

She sees you come in, Daddy.
There is always a set of eyes on you.

THE STINK

That summer the stink grew and rose through a heat wave that left everyone in the city sticky with sweat. Keith, the guy I was fucking at the time, liked to ask me about women we knew and if I could imagine being with them. He said their names and usually I said, "Yes." I found almost everyone on the planet attractive during that time. He made me feel like, with all the people I'd been with, I was just some splintery board waiting to be rubbed up against. Keith liked to watch me touch myself, and he told me to tell him what I was thinking about. He said it turned him on. From this we learned that every day there was something new I found erotic. He told me that whatever was sexy to me was sexy to him and we made our fantasies that way, at least until he got sick of me.

One day he said, "Melissa?"

And I said, "I don't know who that is," but of course I did.

I got him to describe her to me. He told me about how she was tall, taller than me by almost a head. He told me what he thought her breast size was and probably exaggerated, but stuff like that didn't bother me. "I fucked her once," he said, but I always knew when Keith was lying from the pinch in his cheeks that meant a smile was coming that never fully did. Then we made up a scenario about the lingerie store where she worked. It was too expensive for me; I was still bartending at the bar next to the store and people tipped me in gossip rather than money. In the lingerie store, according to Keith's fantasy, the saleswomen had to model the lingerie and customers ended up making out or having full-blown sex in the change rooms. I climbed on top of him as he spoke, begged him to keep talking, but even after just hearing the name Melissa I was ready to go.

Really, I couldn't imagine there was a woman out there who was more perfect than me. I was barely twenty-six, and I swelled with the power of my attractiveness. People started to secretly say I was conceited, but I had ears and I knew what they were chatting about. I also knew enough by then to know that people liked to think someone who loved their body was vain; it was the same thing they thought about Melissa. To be accepting of yourself gave you power and one of the ways to stomp on someone's power was to pretend its source was something disgusting. I saw it in Melissa and liked it, and I liked it in myself. Everyone else didn't know anything—they just knew how to move their mouths until they were tired or thirsty and then ordered another drink from me.

Customers complained about the stink. It coated their tongues, so they thought something was off in their drinks. The AC was also spotty. I'd journey into the basement and play with the settings, kick at that damn machine. Sometimes it started humming away and everyone clapped as I climbed back up, as if I'd fought off a monster down there, delivered everyone from certain doom. But we were already stuck to the roof of a dead dog's mouth, everything hot and rancid and damp.

Eventually the customers called my boss about the stink, even though it wasn't just in our bar, the stink was everywhere, under the shade of the trees and along the boardwalk, especially directly under the sun, which glowed bright and red and deep. Sunsets and sunrises seemed to stay still and hovered all early morning and evening. Time in general slid slowly around the clock. My boss ordered me to take out the garbage on the hour.

The garbage bins had less sludge in their bottoms if I took them out often, fewer beer bottles with glass shards to slice the bags open and release the slurry of food and old booze on me. Outside, in the alley behind all the stores and restaurants, Melissa was smoking on break from the lingerie store. I dumped the garbage. "Hi," I said to her. The stink rose from the row of garbage cans. My boss kept adding more cans, thinking it would disperse the smell. I stared at Melissa, although I didn't mean to. I couldn't get Keith's sexy scenarios out of my head. She just waved at me and didn't say anything. Crushed her cigarette against the brick of the building and went inside.

Melissa kept getting creepy messages from different Twitter accounts. Everyone was talking about it. Keith had an almost photographic memory for language, so he'd say the Tweets to me from memory as we fucked. All I'd say was "I'm Melissa." It was a game we played, one last-ditch attempt to excite each other before we lost interest.

After we had sex three or four times and were both exhausted, Keith fell asleep beside me. His breathing whistled and his hand held my wrist as he slept. I hoped he wouldn't forget me after we moved on. "Who's tweeting at Melissa?" I asked him when he stirred.

It was dark and the heat held us in such a way that we couldn't move. "I think I might be in love with her," he said. "I talk to her from time to time."

"Fine." It was too hot for me to give myself fully over to Keith. "Don't forget to tell me about it later."

When I hadn't heard from Keith in a week, I found Bryant. He was slouched in a chair outside a coffee shop. "Well, hi," I said to him, kicking at his shoe. He looked at me with these great eyes as if someone had taken a mirror and smashed it and tried to put it back together all wrong. I knew exactly who he was. When he and Melissa started dating back when they were twenty, people said they'd never seen a couple so in love. I looked to see if Melissa was inside, to see if this might finally give her a reason to talk to me. But he was alone, as he was most times I saw him around. On his wrist, he'd gotten *Mel* tattooed in what everyone said was her cursive. I fell down into the chair beside him and introduced myself. He handed me a cigarette.

I got him laughing telling him about some of the gossip I heard behind the bar and told him I had half a bottle of wine at home. We started walking and goofing around. He stopped to bat at my ass every couple of steps. Even though I wasn't Melissa, he wanted me. After we had sex, he buried his face into my curly hair, and I asked him if we could keep fucking. I'd heard Melissa was more or less done with him.

"Are you sad you're breaking up?" I asked him.

"Everyone thinks she's perfect, but she's not," he said. "I was with the woman for five years. It's totally different when you're with a woman like that." His whole face twitched. I wasn't sure if it was from exhaustion, sadness, disgust. "It'll be good. It'll be good when it's over."

I didn't expect them to patch things up, but they did. I kept fucking Bryant.

After the air conditioning of Melissa's place, Bryant couldn't stand the heat of mine. I set up three fans to be ready for him the next time he came over, one facing the bed and another on a TV table I used as a desk and another beside the hot plate. On their highest settings, they created a breeze, even though they stirred up the stink. My apartment was above a fruit stand that always stank during the summers anyway. Nothing but the smell of rot, but it was a short walk to work and barely cost me anything.

Keith stopped by the bar to return a couple of paperbacks I'd given him. "I dropped one in the bath," he said. "I hope that's okay." I asked him if he wanted to fuck in the backroom. The bar was deserted.

"I can't," he said, and ordered a Dark 'n' Stormy.

I was glad to have him stay and chat. I wanted to catch up, but he didn't have all that much to say. I told him not to tell anyone, but I'd been fucking Bryant even though he'd gotten back with Melissa. That I didn't even really hope he'd leave or want to be with him, just liked sharing something with her.

Keith finished his drink in one quick sip. "I don't know. He's not a good guy, from what I hear."

"Who'd you hear that from? Melissa? That's not what I've heard. And they're back together, so why'd you think that? What do you know?"

Keith shook his head and put money on the bar.

Most days, Bryant didn't come close to Keith. There was something about the way all those little shards of mirror in his eyes could flip around that brought this hardness to him, especially as we fucked. It was those times when I could most slip into the fantasy that I was Melissa. It worked in the moment to send me over the edge, but after he left, I sat on my bed with a book with both covers torn off. They call a book like that a stripped book because it can't be sold, I guess. I ran its frayed pages underneath my fingernails. It wasn't shame I was feeling, more like a troubling stillness and a fear that I was destroying myself. In the shower I scrubbed at my skin, the stench even heavier with the steam.

My bedsheets were still wet from our sex. I combed through my closet, pushing aside old winter coats, looking for another fan I was sure I had. My hands were slow and clumsy and my hair slapped my shoulders with its wetness as I moved.

I picked up a bicycle helmet and garden tools and let them slip from my fingers and pawed at a windbreaker I'd forgotten I had and cut the side of my hand on the claw of a hammer. Blood gushed over the inside of the closet, onto the extension cords and power bars and instruction manuals. I put my hand to my mouth and sucked. The taste of my blood made me gag. I grabbed a towel and wound it around my hand. It stained quick, but stayed in place, soaking up the mess coming out of me. I decided not to strip the sheets. I was too tired and everything was damp and smelled and was surrounded by the damn heat anyway, so it didn't matter what I did. Why strip sheets to just need to strip them again in the morning?

I don't know how I knew, lying in my bed with my damp sheets stuck to my legs and my hand wrapped in that bloody towel, but when I woke up, before doing anything I checked my Twitter feed and then I checked Melissa's. Someone had hacked into her account and written *Im comin for you Melissa. Your family too.* And another. *I will kill you bitch.* The stink made me retch that morning, especially as I washed my towel in the sink. The blood clung like rust along the bottom of the drain. I breathed in and out slowly, trying to keep down last night's wine. I'd seen Melissa outside at least once a day when I emptied the trash. Sometimes I even bummed a smoke from her. The blood in the sink reminded me of the alley's brick wall, her crushed cigarettes. I needed to say something to her. I wondered if she was scared.

At work, I poured drinks and dunked deep-fried pickles and chicken wings and counted down until the hour was up and I could see Melissa. When I went out to the alley, she was smoking and crying quietly, staring into the sun that hung there like it hated us.

"I saw everything online. You okay?" I dumped the trash.

"I don't give a shit about that," she said. "My dad had a heart attack."

"Oh," I said, and moved closer to her. She was the only one in this city who didn't smell. Close to her, I filled my nostrils. I wanted her smell to cover me, but as soon as I stepped away, that stink set back into me. It was in my pores. Whenever I showered, I waited for the water to get scalding hot to burn away the stench, but it was in the water too. Putrid. Rot. Maybe all the water in the world had gone bad somehow and no one had noticed yet. Melissa had water stored in her basement while the rest of us washed our bodies with the rank liquid that spewed from our faucets. "Did you just hear?"

She nodded and glared up at the sky again, sucking on her cigarette. "I'm out of this fucking place," she said. She was wearing a tank top, and a shimmer of sweat clung to her skin. She was so close. With the back of my fingers, I ran my hand over her, skimming the sweat away. I cupped my hand around her shoulder, felt her skin burning underneath.

"I'm going to miss you," I said.

She moved my hand off her, but her fingers took their time as they pushed against my skin.

That night when Bryant came over, I didn't pretend I was Melissa. I couldn't get into it. I thought of her crying in the alley, and I lay there like a blow-up doll.

"What's the matter with you?" he said, and shook me. "Don't you want to fuck?" He held his hard dick in his hand and pumped it over me.

"It's too hot," I said, and rolled over onto my stomach. "Everything stinks."

"Don't you have another fan around here?" The three hummed in unison, waving their heads back and forth.

"In the closet."

Bryant pulled open the closet door, and he screamed high and long, not like I thought a man would scream, but like a dog, kicked deep in the stomach. "What the hell!"

I dragged myself from the bed and walked to the closet, naked. He was staring at its insides. Blood was everywhere. Over the walls and the cords and smeared on the door handle.

"What did you do?" he asked me. The mirror pieces all flipped to their reflective sides, light glinting everywhere. "What the fuck did you do?"

I laughed and laughed. I held up my hand. "I cut myself by accident," I said. "I must've forgot."

"It stinks. It stinks like blood in here. Nasty," he said. "I'm going home."

"Don't you know she's gone?" I said. Bryant was pulling on his pants. "She's left the city, Bryant."

"What?" he said.

"She left. Her dad had a heart attack."

"Her dad?" He paused with one arm in his T-shirt before his hand burst through the sleeve. "Why'd she tell you?"

I just smiled at him and shrugged, as though I knew everything that would ever happen in his life and didn't care much about any of it.

He slammed his fist into the wall beside my head. I started shaking, but there was nothing he could do to me. "You're scared?" he said, rubbing his hand.

I tried calling Keith after Bryant was gone, but a voice said his number was unavailable. For the rest of the week, I looked for him all over the city. But I was alone, with only the city's whispers.

Keith came back to the city and showed up at the bar. He put both elbows on the counter and ordered a Dark 'n' Stormy. Nobody drank those anymore. He told me that, for a while, he'd moved with Melissa to her hometown, and the air was cool and clear, but eventually the heat found him there too.

"What was it like being with her?" I asked. "Was it like we imagined?"

He shoved his hands into his hair, which already stuck to his forehead. They trembled as he put them back around his glass, a habit he'd later learn to conceal. "It was a complete nightmare," he said.

I left Keith to watch the bar and descended the steps to the basement to check the AC. Even down there it was foul and hot. I flicked dials and switches and fuses, kicked and hollered and begged, I wrapped my body around the machine. The more I moved, the more I stank. The cold would never come.

THERE'S NO MORE HAPPINESS LEFT

JOY

Sam stretches out her legs under the blanket, and this gives her joy. There is a warm body beside her, his back pressing against her arm like a gentle cat, and this gives her joy. The bedroom feels like a secret clubhouse because Travis is there, and it's snowing outside but warm inside, and this gives her joy. But it's time to get out of bed, and she knows there's nothing that can ruin this joy, not today. It's morning and nothing can shake the joy out of her.

It's a wonderful time to be young. To put coffee on, listening to the water boil, smelling the grounds, watching as the water splashes through and turns dry to sog, to a dark brown liquid with a bit of golden froth. And then waiting just the perfect amount of time for it to steep, just enough time to do a dish or two and look out the window as snow falls down. The ground isn't white yet. Her mind tries to freeze on each individual flake, but, like her, they fall too fast.

He stretches in the bedroom. She can hear him groan. Her pyjama pants drop to the floor, as if pulled down by the sound of him waking instead of her own hands. She pulls her T-shirt off, sets it silently down. He calls for her. She forgets about the coffee and runs and jumps onto the bed, where he is swaddled in the comforter.

Tim asks her what her worst nightmare is. She smiles and deflects. He says, "Like, I want to know what your version of hell is." He holds her wrists as he says this, but not as though he wants to control her, that won't happen until he's older. They are stretched out, the entire length of the sofa. The way he's holding her wrists, one in each of his hands, it's more like he thinks she might fade away in a second, like if he doesn't keep a part of himself joined to a part of her, she will be gone, and he'll be alone on the couch again playing video games.

"Tell me yours," she says.

"No, I asked you."

"For me, it's a place where love doesn't exist. And it's hot and smells, and people just keep using each other up, and there is no happiness, none at all. Only, like, a discomfort. Like your skin is too tight for your body."

He runs his hands up under her shirt and over her stomach. "Too tight for your body?" he laughs, and she laughs too, squirms closer to him. She imagines their bodies are two halves of a worm wanting to be reattached. Just two weeks ago, he'd never touched her skin, only the skin of her lips on his lips, and now he touches all of it, and she touches all of it.

"Too tight for your body," she says back, and runs a finger along his arm.

"In my hell, people can't stop arguing," he says.

"Arguing? That's all you got?"

"Well, sometimes they just argue and sometimes they hurt each other. They stab and punch, but no one can die. And they just don't leave each other alone. They have to keep arguing again."

She thinks this might be about his parents. She holds him to her. "My hell is a city," she says, her mouth now sitting against his collarbone. "A city where you go because you think it's where you're supposed to go, but then when you get there everyone is cruel and hurts each other. Sometimes kill each other. A city where sometimes you wake up and you don't even know what happened."

His hands are now around the back band of her shorts. His fingers play with each belt loop. Even her clothes are fascinating to his body. "My hell is being stuck in a box and you know you are in a box, and it's dark and everyone knows you're there and no one will help you out."

"My hell is an elevator ride that never ends."

"My hell is infinite trips to the hardware store."

"I thought you liked going to the hardware store with your dad."

"Changed my mind."

"Really?"

"My hell is not being allowed to change my mind."

"Okay, okay."

Then she says, "My hell is a world without you," because she knows that's what he wanted to hear all along. He eye-smiles down into her eyes, which eye-smile back. Their lips are so close that they are barely not touching, noses jammed together.

"Do you want to?" he says to her.

"Yes," she says.

HUG

Mommy and Daddy are hugging in the kitchen. Kylie says, "Me too!" She shoves herself in between. Mommy on one side, Daddy on the other side. Daddy's stomach smooshed against her face. Mommy warm, against her back.

Her brother, Tim, watches from the kitchen door, smiling. Sometimes he joins, tries to get in the middle too. Or he wraps his body around the three of them, as much as he can. His arms are still so small. But many times, he catches himself, remains outside.

Mommy and Daddy kiss over the top of Kylie's head. Their bodies make a roof. "Squeeze," Kylie says, and her parents squeeze.

Kylie feels herself uncoil. *This is my home*, she thinks.

"Enough," Mommy says. "Daddy and I need some time together."

Kylie joins Tim at the kitchen door, and they watch their parents kiss.

"Gross," Kylie says, and her brother nods. They go off to play.

GOOD TOUCHES

The plastic from a bag from the discount bookstore digs into Sam's hand. Both she and Kylie had agreed that they needed to buy books urgently. "To ease the discomfort of being alive," Kylie had said.

"Exactly," Sam had agreed.

Now they sit on the curb in front of an elementary school, still empty though summer is nearing its end. Sam runs her hand through the grass. They lay their books out on the ground.

"I love sitting on a curb like this," Kylie says. "It reminds me of being in high school with nothing to do, nowhere to go."

"I hated high school," Sam says. "I wanted to be like we are now."

"Except you didn't know it'd be so depressing."

"Exactly."

Sam hands Kylie her books one by one. Kylie admires her purchases, celebrates her good taste. Sam looks at Kylie's books and reads their back covers. She tries to focus on talking about books. Kylie turns one of Sam's over in her hands, *Ten Ways to Be Happier*. The book is for Travis. Sam finally says, "I think we're gonna break up again." She begins to talk about how difficult it is to be with someone who has a completely different moral code than she does, someone who doesn't even think about having a moral code at all. She wants Travis to not hate himself the way he does, but she can't help him. She doesn't know how to communicate with him, with anyone. She doesn't tell Kylie that sometimes, in the middle of the night, Travis begs her to get married, but then their days in Toronto are full of the chaotic loneliness that only comes from being with someone not-quite-right.

Kylie listens. She pats Sam on her shoulder first. Sam begins to cry. Running her hand along where Sam's bra strap presses into her skin, Kylie presses on a knot of tension in Sam's back. *How did she know?* Sam thinks. *How did she know I'm always hurting there?* It's different to be around someone who understands your aches. "It's like, I knew I could put a few years into this and it might not turn into anything, but now what do I have?"

Kylie presses harder. "No, Sam, you don't understand," Kylie says. "There is so much good in your life."

BAD TOUCHES

It happens at a work meeting. To Kylie, all touches are created equal. To Kylie, it feels as if all of her is a sex organ, ready to be stimulated at any time. She is ashamed of this.

The team is discussing the negotiation of a new contract. Kylie has stuck chart paper up on the wall. She likes seeing ideas posted up, likes seeing the way words look on paper. Kylie wants to be in charge because she likes the way her voice sounds when she gets really serious. It's different than when she talks to her friends, always lilting up, always begging to be liked. Kylie is wearing high-heeled ankle boots with laces. She feels proud when she laces them standing up. Only she knows all the effort it takes to balance.

The woman at the meeting is Kylie's senior. Soon it's her voice that is really serious. Kylie's voice begins to morph into up-talk. She even accidentally swears when she's getting flustered. The woman chastises Kylie, playfully. "We didn't know you had it in you," she says, which in the woman's mind is a compliment, meaning that Kylie is usually on her best behaviour and it's neat that she's getting a little looser.

It makes Kylie think of this: when she was in Grade 1 she went to the bathroom by herself because she was in a Grade 1/2 split, so unlike the other Grade 1s, the students didn't have to go in partners. She sat on the toilet swinging her legs as she waited for the poop to be ready to fall from her. Sometimes she'd push, but it kind of hurt, so mostly she waited. Then she washed her hands and walked back to class.

"Kylie, what took so long?" her teacher said.

"I was going BM," Kylie said. The whole class began to laugh.

"Kylie! That is too much information!"

The class laughed louder. Kylie returned to her seat, humiliated.

This is what the woman is doing to her. Kylie's scalp begins to prickle with rage, a big smile still on her face.

If she focuses on the work, it's easier. At the front of the room, the woman continues to take charge. Kylie grabs a marker and stands beside her, beside the chart paper that was her idea. And then it happens. The woman ducks around behind her, and her hand presses in the dip right above her butt. Kylie knows how to deflect the woman's touch without it seeming rude—she's had many years of practice. It's as though her whole body is involuntarily inverting, her back arches, and she steps forward and writes something on the paper, an idea she'd been trying to say but the woman kept talking over her. To the woman, her touch has not even occurred. She was only moving people around, the way she is used to doing. Kylie's heart is smashing against her lungs. In a few minutes, she takes a bathroom break.

In the bathroom, Kylie thinks about her breasts and she thinks about her butt and she imagines that she is nothing but a mind. A mind that is maybe attached to a robot. A robot that can feel no sensations, only carry out tasks. Despite Kylie's messy twenties, her thirty-year-old self tries most days to be like this. *One day, the world will end and there will only be cyborgs*, she thinks. *And then I'll be okay.*

MOUTHS IN HELL

The streetcar is full of mouths, and Tim's mouth tastes like cheeseburger. His hand spreads on the small of his daughter's back, to steady her. He sucks the inside of his cheek, wishing he had a mint.

Two young girls sit with their feet on the seats and their legs folded into their chests. Their mouths press to their knees. Mouths beside them talk into phones. A man beside him accidentally shoves his electric guitar right into Tim's shin. Then the man's mouth smirks. A woman to Tim's other side licks her lips. "Do you have your money?" Tim asks his daughter. "Do you have your ticket? Do you have your purse?"

"Yes, I have everything," she says, and fishes her phone out of her pocket and begins to text her friend. *streetcar taking forever*, Tim reads over her shoulder. *My dads freakin out*

he mad?

I think hes just worried for no reason. She puts a crying-with-laughter emoji.

Ten minutes ago, they were sitting across from each other at a restaurant while she rattled off facts about the band she was going to see tonight. She'd told him again and again thank you for taking her downtown, for the tickets, for letting her go alone with her friend once he drops her off. He moves his hand slightly up as the streetcar rocks.

"God, Dad," she says, batting his hand away. "I wish you wouldn't do that."

ROUTINE

Sam is having a nightmare. She's never lived a life at all. She was only dreamed into existence by one of the people she had sex with. Only the encounter had made her real. The heat from his face, the salty taste of his fingers, the brush of his eyelash, the magic feeling of someone else's breath against you, or someone's eyes blinking against your skin. In her dream, she approaches climax again and again, and the person, he doesn't let her, he teases her, he says he's not sure she wants it. The moment before she wakes up fully, Sam is certain she has died. Possibly has been murdered by Travis—she always had a feeling that one of the men she slept with would be the person to take her life. And then she wakes up and is alone in her apartment. She begins her morning routine: coffee, meditation, stretching, dishes, looking out the window for a prolonged period of time. This routine is the only thing that still makes her happy.

She messages Kylie and tells her all about the dream.

Hmm, Kylie types, *a little on the nose.*

WINTER BANGER

I'd known Nick for three days when he came over to my apartment because he said he was already half in love with me. We'd met at a party, and now here he was at my place. He paced around my apartment as he told me this, and also that he couldn't stop thinking about me, all the time, and he just wanted to be near me if I'd have him. He asked me, "Can I smoke in here? I need to smoke."

"At the window," I said, pointing to the bathroom window above the toilet, even though I knew my roommate would be pissed if she found out. She was in love with the apartment, and I wasn't, and for some reason this made me want to piss her off. I slammed the doors a lot, I went out late and stumbled around loudly when I got home, I let people smoke as long as it was in the bathroom. I didn't want her to feel like the place belonged to her.

Nick was also somebody else's, if somebody can ever really be somebody's, but nothing stopped me. Sometimes it felt as if I were his mouth smoking, that I sucked things in with this unstoppable energy that got both me and everyone around me in trouble. I crowded into the bathroom with him as he smoked, both of us crammed onto a little wooden bench over the radiator underneath the window. I wanted to be as close to him as possible. My hand kept brushing his thigh. I kept checking to see if he had a boner yet.

In the bedroom, he kept his underpants on, he said because of his girlfriend. His dick was hard in his underwear and reaching toward me, and he wrapped his arms around me in a side hug, pushed against my leg with a little moan. I gathered him in my arms as though he were a child a mother had either lost or hated, and either could have been true. I loved him even then, the way his drunken breaths came out in little whistles that tickled my chin. *Shit*, I thought. *I'm doing it again.*

Soon he had a key and he didn't have another girlfriend anymore, and then within a week he didn't even have another place anymore, our lives just collapsed together into one big shit-show. He still smoked at the window in the bathroom since it was the only one without a screen and he could stick his head all the way out. Sometimes he walked around the apartment after flushing the butt down the toilet, trailing snow that had caught in his hair while his head had been stuck out there. He was wonderfully unaware. It was nice to be around someone who barely felt his own existence, who constantly moved, hopping from one foot to the other, passing from room to room before speeding out the door.

My roommate was pissed. Nick and I fucked loudly and against the walls. I thought he'd appeared just to help that friendship move on its natural course. On some level, my room-mate and I hated each other. Or not hated, we were bored, bored by the faux-intimacy the place had forced on us. It wasn't like with my best friend, Sam, whom I spoke with multiple times a day about everything: Nick, the news, our jobs, even random things that interested us for just a moment. Sometimes Sam called to read me an article or a short story over the phone. It was nice, that closeness.

My roommate would stand in our kitchen and ask if Nick had a job. One hand would be holding an apple, and one a knife, and she'd be peeling the apple by turning it against the blade of the knife. When I first met her, I thought it was fantastic. It was so honest, connected to an older way of living. "Why would anyone buy a peeler?" she would say as she peeled an apple or a potato. After living with her for about a year, I was sick of hearing her say this and hid my peelers in the bottom of the second drawer, under her wooden spoons stained from cooking homemade curries and pastas. I barely cooked, but after fishing the peelers out, I'd always look around to make sure she wasn't going to burst into the kitchen and catch me skinning a carrot.

I told her, "No, he's going to school," which is what he'd told me. It was pretty obvious after having him there for a week or two that school meant he hung around the apartment carrying one stack of my books from the bedroom to the kitchen to the living room and back again. He then wrote down ideas he had about the books without reading them carefully. He would read his fragmented thoughts out loud to me in the middle of the night. I hoped my laughter and the sound of Nick's voice would wake my roommate. I hoped the sounds were oppressive.

I had the smaller bedroom, and soon it was covered in a layer of papers with Nick's ideas on them. He would wake me up some mornings and say, "Okay, squirrel, we're going on an adventure," and the adventure would be walking all over the city, ducking into second-hand shops to look for a particular book he wanted. One time he walked out of a commercial bookstore with a whole stack of books. He told me he'd put his wallet on the top of the stack so it looked as if he'd paid. "They shouldn't be charging great thinkers for books anyway," he said. "People like you and me, we should get all of our books for free."

People like you and me. Yes, at that period in time, I hoped Nick and I were the same. I delighted in the quickness of his mind, the way he constantly came up with ideas, how he attributed the same speed and intelligence to me. He told me, "I love how you live," when he first saw my place. "This is one of the reasons I think our souls are destined for each other." He liked my record player and soon bought his own records to play. He liked my desk and the table in the kitchen, which was flanked by windows looking out over the snowy backyard.

Most of all, he liked the recklessness I lived with at that time. That I took my life day by day, as if I was scared I'd wake up and it would all be shattered. I believed this was a problem with me, with my eyes that could never seem to focus on one thing—they were always flitting around tempting men and women, or at least that's how I imagined it. The stalled friendships, betrayals, broken hearts, trauma, and terror, the absolute inability to get an adult life started, all were likely of my own doing. But Nick looked at this rawness and he held it up and said, "You have a really true soul, Kylie. I think you're doing okay." And even before he'd broken up with his girlfriend, he said, "I'm glad the world brought us together."

This was all at the beginning of winter.

Sam and I laugh about it all now. I'll go over to her house, and we'll grab a bottle of wine. We go onto her porch, where she's leaned a ladder against the side of the house so we can climb onto the roof. I get nervous climbing, but Sam guides me as she scrambles up. Usually she'll launch into a story about climbing trees as a child, and then I'll be up on the roof too. We'll stretch out, feel warm under the direct sunlight, and drink. After a glass or two, we'll go:

"Remember when you lived with Nick?"

"Remember when you walked home all the way from the east end because you didn't have any money for a cab or a token? And your feet bled for days?"

"Remember when you had a roommate?"

"Remember that guy from the boat?"

"Oh god, Tight 'n' Bright? I was trying to forget."

It's like a secret code. Really the conversation means: "You have lived through all these bad times, and I was there for you during these bad times and will continue to live and go through your bad times and my own bad times and we will continue to be able to keep going." It's like a prayer for life. But we laugh, getting louder and louder and higher in pitch.

Originally I thought of that party we met at, or at least the way Nick told the story, as if it were a magical night. At the time, I was writing content for different types of blogs. Mostly I'd procrastinate and then stay up all night writing the most inane things… How to Keep Your Garden Bug-Free, Where to Shop for the Best Sunglasses, How to Face the Winter This Season. We made all our money off ad sales, and so I had to name-drop as much as possible, cram each post full of links. I feel that this job contributed to how much I hated myself that year, but it's hard to say, when the hatred has always been there. The guy who managed the ad sales was having the party, and he and I had had a brief fling, so he invited me. And Nick was there.

I quit my job when everything fell apart with Nick, and the ad sales guy offered to let me crash on his couch. I told him, "Fuck no, you're the one who got me in this mess," and found myself telling him the whole story about meeting Nick at his party in November, and everything that had happened that winter, and now it was May and I was trying to get my damn life together for once. The ad sales guy said he had no idea who I was even talking about, so there was that. Perhaps Nick's girlfriend had lived in the building and he had just come down the stairs and into the open apartment where the music was coming from. It was definitely something he would do.

At the party, Nick had grabbed my hand as I pulled a scoop of punch up out of the bowl, trying not to spill on the way to my glass. "Don't drop any!" he'd said, shaking my hand. "Look how you tremble!" At the time, this charmed me hard. Later, as I pushed his things into boxes asking him to, please, get out quickly, he said it to me again with the same laugh: "Look how you tremble."

Man, my roommate couldn't get out of there fast enough. She told me Nick was already there all the time, that he could take over her share of the lease and she was going to move back in with her parents. I said, "You think I'm really going to go onto a lease with him?"

My roommate said, as she started to gather the books that were hers from the kitchen table, from the bookshelves, trying to hold them all at once in her crossed arms, "You're acting like I want to go live with my parents when one day he was just living here. I just can't live with you guys anymore. I can't stand the noise, having someone else around. You moved him in without even discussing it with me, really."

"It just happened," I said, but I started to help her pick out which books were hers before she went into her room.

Nick was in mine. "What did that bitch want?" he asked.

There was one night that was special, when I woke up in the dark after dreaming my own death. Nick listened to me describe the dream, and he told me about how he'd feared death too, until he saw a dead body when he was eighteen. That it was just lying there in the forest behind his house, and he realized that he was only a body too, so what did it matter to get all worked up about something we were all going to go through. People had done it before, so it had to be fine.

Sam told me later that she'd seen the dead-body thing he'd described in a movie. Nick liked to pretend things he read or saw were real sometimes. Sam said it was to trick me, to make me think he was wiser and more feeling than he was, but I still liked to see it as a hopeful Nick, saying, "It had to be fine."

I didn't understand that Nick was someone who always needed an enemy. That probably, at one time, it was his girlfriend, and then it was my roommate, and then once the roommate was gone, and it was only the two of us together, it was me. Winter is the time for a couple to cling together, to watch TV and read in the same room silently, but once it warmed up, he only wanted to be outside, and he definitely didn't want to be with me. What was worse was that I was a human being who sweated and liked attention and expected to keep that cozy winter vibe. It wore me down: "bitch" now directed at me, cold glances, how he left the room when I entered, or was always on his cell texting someone else.

We'd been out walking with Sam, and he kept walking ahead of us, not wanting to walk with us. Sam tried to cheer me up, saying we were a cute couple, and he said, "She's been all right. A good winter banger." The day ended with us alone at home in bed, sweaty from the strange, early-May heat wave and tired from walking. My hair had frizzed up from the humidity and I stared at myself in the mirror, patting at it. I used to joke with Sam that my hair, which grew and shrunk in different temperatures, was where I stored my power. I kind of believed it, but Nick didn't.

"Your hair's all wrong," he said. "I wish it was flat, sleek. Straighten it. Go straighten it." It wouldn't matter if I plugged in the straightener, waited for its heat to try to flatten the hair that would never sit down even if I spent an hour on it. He didn't want me as I was. And who would ever want me, the way I was, all wrong, inside and out? Even inviting Nick into bed with me in the first place had been wrong. I always wondered how I could be so stupid to not realize I needed to be alone.

I started to cry, big sloppy tears the way I'd always cried

since I was a kid, throat tight and burning, choking as though he had his hands right around my neck, hating myself, inside and out, inside and out, anything I hated about the world turned in on me, part of me. I couldn't hold anything against Nick—he was just clearly articulating his preferences, asserting what I knew to be true, that I'd never be enough.

"Don't cry," he said, and he pulled me on top of him. I cried even harder. He pulled me down, wrapped his arms around my body, pressed his forehead to mine. My tears fell onto him. He smoothed my hair with his hands, pressing it against the side of my head. "Don't cry." And then he started to kiss me and press his crotch into me. I could feel his dick harden underneath my hips. He was pulling at my pants and pressing his dick into my vagina, and it had been so long since we'd had sex, it hurt, but I think I wanted it. I wanted sex all the time and we never had it.

He came after a minute or two and pushed me off him. As I always felt after he came, I was calm, reassured, but something else was also happening to me. The skin on my cheeks was tightening as the salt water dried there. I tried to brush the water away, but it was already gone. Nick, too, was getting up and pulling on a hoodie, grabbing a cigarette packet from the top of my broken bookshelf and checking to see if there were any left.

As usual after he went outside to smoke and wander, I started to touch myself, trying to get off on my clit, but this time I couldn't come. I thought back to when I first met Nick. That party. I'd been a fool. He knew he had to get out of his girlfriend's place, he knew he could get into mine, that he could keep going on the way he always did, shack up with his winter banger, and then, in a little bit, once he found his next girlfriend, he'd be gone again.

I went into the shower and turned it on to full heat. I peeled my shirt off and stepped into the steam and water, let it hit my back, my face. I started crying again. I looked up and saw the rod holding the shower curtain, and I made a plan. I would hang myself from the rod. I just needed a rope, and then I would have a way out.

As I stepped out of the shower, I tugged affectionately at my escape. The rod came down on my head lightly, then bounced off. The curtain dragged against my body as its plastic curled in on itself, pulling over my skin like a wet tongue. I pushed the curtain off me angrily. I punched at it and I almost fell over as my fist pushed the curtain aside. I kicked at it. "Get the fuck out of my way," I said to the stupid curtain and examined where the rod had been. There wasn't even a mark. I picked the rod up and it was light and flimsy. I smacked it against the wall and listened to it ping.

I'd always thought everything in the apartment was permanent: my roommate, Nick, me, the rod that held up the curtain. But it was only a tension rod. To make it smaller, all you had to do was twist it one way. To tighten it against the wall, twist the other way.

I called Sam. I wanted to tell her what had happened. Instead, I said, "Nick is being a jerk again," and she told me to come over. I picked out my clothes slowly and methodically. I dressed. I went back into the bathroom. The curtain was draped over almost everything. I picked it up and slid it onto the rod, which I pressed against the tiled shower walls until it sat snuggly, the curtain back in place. I wiped the water from the floor with a towel. It was as though nothing had ever happened in there or could ever happen. I even replaced the empty toilet paper roll before I left, promising myself it would be the last time.

I looked at ten places before I found my apartment, on the second floor of a house. It's newly renovated, no memories haunting it. Just my apartment. It's not for me to share with anyone, at least not yet. Sometimes I take a stack of books and I move them from the bedroom to the kitchen to a little nook where I've set up a reading chair. I keep my peeler on the counter and cook more. Through the back window, the trees have gone to bud. Through the front, people move along the sidewalk, duck in and out from a café across the street. I'd always thought my roommate had been dumb, falling in love with that apartment we'd shared. But now I'm here, and I'm alone, and hell yeah, I'm in love.

You have eyes of your own.
They find grates, gaps in doors, peepholes.

THE PUBERTY
DRAWER

We are sitting around a table at the bar talking about what I call the puberty drawer. My—well, let's call him the man I love? My very best friend? The person I'm seeing? We don't use the words *boyfriend* or *girlfriend*, which I say is because we think labels are stupid, although secretly I think it might be because he's ashamed of me. Or not ashamed, just feels like every day he can't believe he's with such a dork. Anyway, my guy's asking questions the way he always does, questions about sex. A couple of the guys laugh awkwardly when the women say anything about—gasp—masturbating, although they share their own stories freely. My guy doesn't laugh like that. He laughs as though nothing you say could ever surprise him, a laugh of acknowledgement and acceptance, and this is one of the things I love about him. He's separated the shame from my past experiences. It seems like very few people in your life can do that for you.

I am the one who brings up the puberty drawer. "The puberty drawer is where you stash all the gross stuff that you did or that happened to you when you were first becoming a juicy teen," I say. "A juicy teen is when you're just at the age that oil starts glistening on your forehead, all your pores are filled with juice, and you're so revved up but haven't had any sexual experiences so that even if someone brushes your arm, you're ready to explode!" I slap the table when I say *explode*.

"So it's an actual drawer?" says one of the guys.

My guy hits his head with his hand in exasperation. "You have to listen," he says. "Of course it's not an actual drawer."

"It's the drawer where you put all those things you don't want to talk about, you never thought you'd talk about, and what you feel like no one will understand. You close it up tight and just skim over those years, get it?"

"Kinda," the guy says.

"Let's open the drawer!" my one friend says.

"Yeah," says my guy, "that sounds like fun."

When I was young, no one ever talked about making themselves feel good. Especially girls. Now that I'm in my thirties, that seems ridiculous. That's all we should have been talking about! Instead we've grown up into people who're all messed—okay, we're not messed, I guess, not in the sense people think, like, I know, I know, we're lucky. We have many things we want and few real problems, but almost everyone I know cries all the damn time. We put ourselves in situations that make us miserable, such as terrible boyfriends, stupid jobs, or life-sucking master's degrees. Some of us have gone through divorces, long-distance moves, child-rearing, and other things we label "the work of life." If only we'd learned to talk about and celebrate things that make us feel good. You know what makes me feel good? Paying my bills! Doing my taxes! Completing short, goal-orientated tasks. I should have been an accountant, like my guy, instead of playing in a vague land of words and ideas where goals are slippery and never really met. (I'm not going to even bother talking about my job because it will depress us both.)

My friend's husband throws back his beer, some of the foam sticking to his whiskers. "Hey, what about those little McDonald's toys?" he says.

My friend says, "Oh, I remember those. I had one that

vibrated and I used that for a while. It was a little purple Furby."

Her husband says, "I put one on my testicles," and puts his arm around his wife like *I'm-so-happy-we're-the-same.*

My guy says, "Seriously? Your balls? That got you off?" although two months later I'll manage to make him come like this with a vibrator. My guy excuses himself to go to the bathroom and limps away.

"Why does Brad have a limp?" one of the guys says. "Is he pinching a dookie?"

"It's an affectation," my friend's husband says.

"I think his foot is just asleep," I say, always quick to jump to his defence. In these moments, I shamelessly expose myself: I'll let no harsh words be spoken about him: I feel his sensitivity, which he often hides, is worth protecting. I show all my friends how much I love him, and become who I truly am: a fool.

I order a drink called Dealer's Choice, which means the bartender will create something for me based on my preferences. The waiter brings a pink goblet of elderberry gin and something sweet with thick white foam on top. It tastes just like dish soap, and we all toast my bad decision. My guy comes back and dunks his fingertip in the white froth, calls me my nickname, Sobs, as in *Here's-Sam-rolling-out-another-sad-story-again*, and shakes his head.

"Okay, I don't know if I should tell you guys this," I say, which I always say when I'm going to tell people something I'll regret later. Whenever I do this, I wake up the next day feeling sick and a little as though I need to either die or crawl back into a womb to be reborn to try to do things right this time. My guy tells me my openness is one of my best qualities, and I think we both hope that, over time, I will outgrow this feeling.

I think, for many girls, we get crushes early, but find our first loves in what I'll call Objects of Our Grinding. Our OOGs. For some, it's a comforter, for others a pillow or the edge of a couch. I was drawn to any stuffed animal with a nose that could press up against my clit, sometimes so hard it made me bleed. The problem with these OOGs for most juicy teens is that the more juiced up you get, the more you need. Every sexual act becomes not enough pretty quickly because what you want is real sex, but you're too young, too scared, or, if you're like me, you just can't find anyone to have sex with.

I always was horniest after swimming in the pool and my nipples became cold and hard. One day my nipples brought me to the basement playroom.

The playroom was where we shoved forgotten toys and books. There was a deadbolt on the door from the previous owner, the only lock in the house. Sometimes my sister and I joked about the lock, whispered about it, made up stories about its origin. When we were a little older, a friend of my sister said he could sense something bad had happened in that room a long time ago. I'd felt guilty, not knowing if it was something I did or something from the previous owner. Our mother had told us that a woman had lived in the basement with a young baby and no husband and her parents. I imagined her father was abusive and so she had the lock put in to protect herself and the baby while he yelled and yelled on the outside. My father yelled, but most times his anger simmered, quietly, waiting. Anyway—that playroom was the site of many explorations for me.

My sister was playing Dance Dance Revolution in the TV room in the basement, and I snuck away after changing from my swimsuit into clothes and still feeling… I'm not really sure. It's still that way for me. Being turned on is often a feeling closely linked to boredom and curiosity. What's over there? What will happen if I do this? And then once things get started, that's when it takes off into real physical sensation. I was so bored and pumping with juice. We weren't allowed to close the playroom door or lock it, and we never did. In there alone, I closed the door almost all the way, sure I'd still be able to hear the heavy steps of a parent coming down the stairs.

I dug through old toys in the closet, looking for something to hump. I wanted something bigger than the old teddy bear I'd been using, one of my first loves, Norman. I wanted something closer to being real. And then I found him—Spot. He was a giant stuffed Dalmatian almost as tall as a short man when spread to his full length. He was stuffed with Styrofoam pellets, which gave his body extra resistance and compacted into hard mounds in the right places. His red tongue had rough edges where the felt had been sealed with glue, and he was perfect. Even more perfect was that for a whole school year, when I was in Grade 1, I brought Spot to school, insisting to others he was an exchange student and needed his own desk. I don't know why teachers let me get away with stuff like that—I was always pushing the limits of what was real and what was allowed to be fantasy. So Spot, in my head, already had some life in him—he'd been educated, after all! He was my perfect new lover.

I pulled off my pants—I'd already progressed far beyond pants-on grinding—and pulled up my shirt and bra. My nipples were far more sensitive than anything below the waist. I pushed him down against the floor and mounted him. His tongue rubbed against my nipples and, for once, my brain totally turned off. I called him Sebastian in my head.

When I was young, I looked deeply into my desire, and a trap door gave out that led me into a pit of deviant sexual hunger. Often in my fantasies, I was tied up, forced to have sex with rows and rows of men, far from home, away from anywhere my parents could find me. In one, Sebastian kept me locked and chained to a bed because he told me, "Your only use is sex." This was still a fantasy I had, but I found the men I dated, though often dominant, weren't that interested in ropes and knots, in stopping what they were doing to tie me up. Or maybe they didn't want their partner to be a passive sexual vessel, the way I always was in these fantasies. In real life, I was someone who strove for power, even as a kid, bossing around my sister and trying to usurp my father as the head of the family. Only during sex would I freely give my power away.

Anyway, I was in deep with my new OOG. I could feel Spot's Styrofoam pellets stiffen into a hard lump underneath me. "It's real," I told myself over and over as I got closer. "You are really having sex."

I heard Dance Dance Revolution pause. My sister had to walk by the playroom to get to the bathroom, but I was too close to stop. I had to keep going. I turned my head and looked at the door and saw that it had crept open, just enough for my sister to glance into the playroom. When she saw me mounting Spot on the floor, she just shook her head and walked on. By that point, she already knew that her perverted sister was gross, always asking her friends if they knew how many fingers counted as almost-sex or asking the neighbourhood boys if any of them had wet dreams and promising, "It was totally normal," with the understanding of a seasoned sex therapist. The head shake kept me from coming though. When she was back in front of the TV, I came out of the playroom, dressed.

"I'm sorry you had to see that," I said.

"It's fine," she said. She continued to dance, stomping left left, right, jumping, ignoring me.

"I know you do it too."

"Not with our old toys," she said.

"Can you keep watch on the stairs? So I can finish?"

"Seriously?"

"Please. I'll owe you one."

"Fine. Whatever."

I went back into the playroom and closed the door fully.

Rekindled my love with Spot until I had a warm, paralyzing orgasm that took over my whole body.

My friends laugh. My one friend says, "Is there anything you wouldn't tell anyone?"

My guy has heard my Spot story before, but he laughs along too and watches my face when she asks that. There's something about his eyes when he watches me like that—they shift between colours, easing from green into blue-grey, and the grey can become almost black. The first time we really connected, he asked me a bunch of questions like we're asking our friends today. When I answered him honestly, he looked at me, and I still think about his eyes on that first day, moving from one shade to another, chin resting against the palm of his hand, fingers pressed to his cheek, when I beat off sometimes.

Her husband says, "No, there's more—look at her! She's blushing!"

"Well, you'd be blushing too," I say, "if you had just told everyone about having sex with your stuffed toy."

My guy keeps watching my face as the others agree, there's more there, there's more there, but then we move on to other topics of conversation.

When we get home, I pull off my dress and he lies on the bed in his boxers, and we talk about all the stories we've shared that night. Before we fall asleep, when we are both protected by the dark, he says, "I feel like there are some things you may never tell me." Considering the only commitment we've made to each other is to be open and honest in all things, it's a very sad thing to say.

There are so many things I want to tell him. I have dreams in which we talk all night and I tell him everything: that I want to be a mother, that I wish I was more like my father, that I like the idea of being faithful to someone, that I think I could do it. Despite the way my relationships have flamed out—that I've just entered my thirties and have already gone through a divorce—all I want to be is true to someone. I want to tell him that when I was young I'd hoped to grow into a human being who lived without regret and was always true to her feelings, and yet lately, I never am.

If you think the drawer's empty after sitting around and sharing, talking about Spot and toys and what we all used as vibrators—then you're wrong. You haven't been paying attention. "You have to listen," my guy would say. That's the thing about a drawer like that: you can take things out and show them to people, and if you do it enough they might no longer seem like things that need to be shut away. But the drawer is deep. There is always something hiding at the back, behind some socks, or even in a sock, so that even if someone snooped all through your drawer, they might say, "Hmm, nothing unusual here!" Even for the guy I'm seeing, that drawer isn't empty—do you think I'm crazy?

"I'm not sure what you mean," I say.

BITES

The bites run in a line along her thigh, curving toward her pussy. At least, she thinks they are bites. Hopes they are. She doesn't want to think about what else they could possibly be. One of her friends thought she had a genital wart when she had a bump like that. She showed everyone she knew. "Do you think it's an STD?" she asked. "I mean STI. It looks like genital warts. But maybe it's a mole?" She went to a clinic to get the wart frozen off, and eventually they told her it was just an ingrown hair on top of a mole. It's easy to be mistaken.

The bites are red and hard and pus-filled. Or maybe full of venom. For a week, she felt burning across her thighs. She told him about it. She got him to place one of his hands on her thigh. "Do you feel the heat? Does this thigh feel warmer than this one?" He told her he didn't know, and after she talked about it two more times he asked her to stop mentioning it, he was sure she was fine. When she stepped out of the shower a few days later, he pointed at her leg and said, "What the hell is on you?" He told her it probably was just a rash but she should get it checked out. But she didn't. The bites are still there. They hurt when she presses on them.

He likes to bite her. At the back of the neck, where her head connects to her spine, or her shoulder, or her face, the cheek. One time he did it and she was left with a bruise after, but it was different than bruises she'd gotten before because although it was unexpected, the first time he did it she told him, "I like being bitten." Or maybe she told him, "I like biting," because she does. But she doesn't bite him because, unlike her, he doesn't like it if it hurts. He's also concerned about hurting her. Once he asked her when she was drunk if it was too much, and he *was* biting too hard, but it was because he was also drunk. With every bite, her skin puffs up and blossoms. It's like a zit, like the bites along her legs.

She hasn't been able to sleep properly since the bites emerged. They itch too much. She's scared of ripping open her skin in sleep. Her skin tends to scar. The bumps from his biting are dark on her cheeks. So are her zits. They don't fade like other people's. Stay dark and purple against her skin. Or maybe others are just better at hiding these things. She stays awake, wondering where the bites came from. What bit her. It's cold outside; how could so many little things still be alive?

She sat on the ground behind the university garbage shed to cry one day between teaching classes. The ground was wet and covered with pine needles. She was wearing tights. They could have been fleas. Or ants.

She then walked until she found a picnic table in an abandoned part of campus. She sat there too. Breathed until she was calm enough to teach her next class. The table's wood could have been full of ants.

She rides transit back and forth every day. Anything could have bitten her. She brushes up against so many people. Maybe something was in the seats.

She is lying in bed and feels something tickle her forehead. She has the lights on because lately she has been afraid of the dark. She is sure that it is the bites and not the light that keeps her from sleeping. Her fingers pinch at her forehead right where it meets her scalp and a little brown bug squirms between her fingers. It wrestles free from her grip. It bounces along her nightshirt-covered chest. She pinches it again. The bug is flat, reddish brown. She walks over to her garbage can and inspects it under the light. It has tiny legs. It's so small that if it hadn't been crawling across her forehead, she never would have found it. She drops it into the black bag in the bin.

She calls him. "What do bedbugs look like?"

"They're really small. Why?"

"Like small, flat, and reddish brown?"

"I think so."

"I found a bug in my bed. What if I have bedbugs?"

"You don't. It'll be fine."

"This is important. I could have to get a whole new bed."

He listens to her worry for a little bit before changing the subject. He's not a patient person but has learned to be patient with her. He treats her with a tenderness she's not used to. She gets off the phone because she needs to strip her sheets. She looks for evidence of bugs. She throws all her bedding in the washing machine on the sanitary setting. She sits on the bare mattress even though she's still worried about the bugs. She calls him back and tells him that bedbugs can get passed on when people sleep around. He tells her he doesn't want to talk about bedbugs anymore. She doesn't have bedbugs, and he'd love to talk to her about anything, anything else. She knows she's being a little extreme.

If only she could bite herself. Swallow herself in one big gulp. Turn inside out, walk around like that, or fold up and collapse. A disappearing wormhole, a burnt-out star creating a vacuum, one of those moths that you clap your hands onto and then it turns into dust.

She doesn't get any new bites, but her scalp begins to itch.

A boy last week sat on the subway and clawed at his blond hair, dandruff floating away from him, down over the seats. She was so tired from working, she sat beside the itchy boy, who continued to scratch.

That's it. It's lice.

She goes into the bathroom at his place and lifts her hair piece by piece. She only finds dander, no bugs, but her scalp is so itchy she picks at it, at anything that doesn't seem normal.

The bites on her leg have finally started to scab. He's stopped pointing them out. That night, she bends over and points her ass into the air. "Bite me," she says. He bites each ass cheek and gives her a slap before climbing on top of her.

The venom has left her. The bites never itch anymore.

In the dark of his bedroom, she remembers the night she confessed that she always thought something was wrong with her. She runs a hand over the scarring bumps on her thigh, the ones from him on her cheek. He is peaceful, not sleeping. He is one of those people who always believes he is right, and she wants to believe him: there is nothing wrong with her. There are no bedbugs and no lice and it was amazing that there were ever bites at all. That little creatures chose her to feed their bodies that also have nothing wrong with them. Just beings charged with a will to exist and lives so much shorter than hers.

The last time he bites her, she will inflate. Her whole body will puff, she will begin to float, the ground will be distant below her. Over hills and cities and fields and all the people biting each other and inspecting their bumps below and over countries she's never seen before and past missiles launched and smoke in the air. She will keep floating, maybe forever, passing through the thinning ozone layer to where there are only black holes and dust in nothingness.

JUST PERVS

Jill, December 2013

It was cold like this the night I tried to go back to Alex. I begged him through the door that was once our door. I told him I was naked under all my clothes, he just had to take them off. I knew all his cheesy fantasies.

Sometimes he texted to check up on me, but I could tell he never got over the cheating.

If you think you're someone who never could hurt anyone, you're lying. You're someone who has never been outside in the cold, or maybe not even in extreme heat. You've never experienced anything. You haven't had dreams where you were the one who held down your best friend, where you were never gentle, you were never kind, you only knew how to be angry and get what you want.

Tonight the door to the bar is glass, the handle so big, like a wooden log. Inside, the room is twisting full of people, some who might hurt me, some who might take me home, and some who want to be destroyed.

Jenade, 2006

I was thinking about it, Jill, and it makes sense... Like, you know, a soul? When I was little, my mom said, it's your true self, it's the self that God sees, it's what's in you. She said it looked just like me, but it was this ideal me. I liked it when I was little because I wasn't who I wanted to be yet. But the thing about the soul is, I think anyway, that it's actually a thin layer spread across the skin. Think about when your heart gets broken, right? That's your soul hurting, but it's the same burning as when you skin your knee or something. That's why I think, Jill, you don't need to worry about having a soul or not having a soul. You have skin, don't you? Then you have a soul. Feel that? Yeah, it feels good, right? That's because it's me, caressing your soul.

Jill, December 2013

These nights that I wander drunk, looking for someone, anyone, to fuck, I expect to find a part of Jenade lying in front of me on the cold, iced cement. A finger. A shin with an exposed bone. Even a few strands of her thick dark hair.

Jill, 2004

For me, the plays chronicle my several failed attempts at sex. I always come close: the nips of my A-cups are rubbed on a bus where I also witness my first hard dick, for two months I have a boyfriend I give multiple hand jobs and one blow job to, and I try to seduce a boy in my anthropology class by wearing no underwear and flashing him my hip bone every time I grab something out of my baggy pants pocket. All of this is true, but I can never get rides to my friends' houses, and very rarely am I allowed on the internet to chat with boys. On top of that, they say I'm flat as flat as flat, although, at night, I study myself naked and am happy with my tiny tits that I know are growing a little each day.

The plays star the four of us as the animals I know we are. Penny fucks my first love in the music practice room. She's the one who knows about anal before I even get my hands on a penis. Dani sneaks into the bathrooms and watches people pee through the cracks in the stalls, guys or girls, it doesn't matter. Jenade keeps a USB strung around her neck with porn based on her favourite fantasy movies and a video on how to deep-throat. She says she wants to feel it beat against her heart as she runs, but Penny says, "It's not her heart she wants to feel it brush against."

Someone found a page from one of my plays on the ground, and I hadn't even changed our names in it, so the person photocopied it and stuffed it into lockers. People laughed for a bit, but we didn't really care. Actually it was a bonus. Like we've been doing this almost revolutionary thing in secret and now finally it's time for it to be shown to the world. A few of the guys told me they liked the play, the writing, that they kept it by their bed at home and then they laughed and I laughed too. Maddy in science told us, "You guys are just pervs. You're so gross. You're like *dudes*."

"She's just jealous she's not in on it," Penny said after Maddy had torn the play into strips and scattered it all over my desk. "And isn't that perfect? She's right. That's what we are. Just pervs."

Jill, December 2013

I see the woman when I'm eyeing the crowd. She's almost as tall as me, and not many I meet are, and she's thick, strong. Her mouth's wide too with big full lips, not like mine. Everything on me's equally thin, as if any fat in my body was sucked out by the last person who kissed me. Her mouth reminds me of Jenade, but Jenade's skin was darker and she was short and curvy unlike this fair, boxy woman, and the woman's eyes are a sharp blue, like Penny's, as if she's waiting for the moment you are off guard so she can catch and punish you. She's sitting at the bar, sipping her drink as if she might even fuck the straw if no one buys her another.

Her mouth makes me drift over and I order us both a shot. After we do them, her mouth curves into an involuntary smile and she presses her hands to her cheeks as if willing them back down. "Shit," she says. "Tequila always makes me so smiley."

I smile too, and soon we're talking about our nights and where we're from, and I forget to look around the room for a man to take me home.

"Are you alone?" she asks me.

"Yes, are you?"

"No, I came with my boyfriend. You have to meet him. You guys will get along great." She waves her hand in the air and he comes over. He's taller than even the two of us and as wide if we were standing side-by-side.

"Look at us," I say. "We're like a team of giants."

"You're too skinny to be a giant," he says, and orders us another round.

I want to be alone with the woman, but I like the man's attention. He must have been watching us the whole time we were talking, and I am thrilled, stripped.

Jill, 2009

Since Alex and I broke up, Jenade often finds her way to my res room. We skip classes and talk about the ideas we're supposed to be reading about until we eventually fall asleep late at night in the middle of conversation.

Last night, Jenade came over after seeing Chris. He's one of those guys that stares at you right in the eyes as if he was there when you pushed your way out of your mom's womb. Who knows who you are and wants to fuck it out of you. Alex wasn't like that. Alex just wanted to keep me inside a bubble made of his sweaty palms.

Before we fell asleep, Jenade stared at the ceiling and asked me if I ever thought about being choked, if I'd ever done it, and I told her no, but I'd seen it in something I watched and it turned me on and I wanted to try it.

"Oh," she said, and continued looking at the ceiling. I

almost asked her if it was something she did, or if Penny had told her about it, but I never brought up Penny, since she wouldn't talk to me anymore.

"Do you want to try it?" I asked her.

"I don't know."

"We can try it…if you want to see what it's like."

We faced each other sitting up in bed, and I put my hands around her neck. I squeezed and then waited until she grabbed my arms and pulled down at my elbows, freeing my hands from her neck. "What did you think?" I asked.

"It was scary. To be out of breath like that."

"Let me try."

She put her hands around my neck, and her skin felt good against mine. Then she started to squeeze. She was right, it was scary, but I felt something else too. It was as if a box had been built up around me, and this made me feel safe at the same time I felt scared. And then there was that wetness in my underwear and I pushed her hands down from around my neck.

"See?"

"You're right," I said, and we got changed and went to bed.

Another night, Jenade and I had sat on the floor of my res room and talked about trying to live a life that was true. That maybe there was a version of ourselves that was realer than all the others and the best us was still out there for us to discover. But I had just been lying. There wasn't another me out there, and if there was, it was even worse than this me. Jenade fell quickly asleep beside me in my twin bed, where I was wrapped in her arms, her mouth pressed to the back of my neck.

My dream that night was of the future. That I would hurt everyone I'd ever loved. Like Alex. Jenade. Even Penny. I dreamed I would drop out and ruin my life and eventually get a job where I convinced other people to let me take something from them, and I would be good at it. Jenade would disappear from my life, as would the rest of the pervs.

Everything danced in my dreams like shadows on a cave wall, cast by some fire I'll never get to see.

Penny, 2006

So what the hell, are you not straight then? I thought you liked dudes. Have you even told Jenade? Are you guys messing around? I can't believe you've been hiding this all along. We're supposed to be open with each other, that's what being a perv is about. At least Dani isn't a poser. Do everyone a favour and don't tell anyone, especially Jenade. I guarantee she doesn't feel the same. You know when she gets home from school, all she does is look for dick all night. Trust me, you're never going to get any action. I don't even think it matters who with. You're not banging anyone.

Jill, December 2013

We're in the elevator of the man's building, or maybe it's the man and woman's building. I don't know either of their names, and I don't even know if they live together or have known each other long, or if the whole thing about them being a couple is a ruse. Maybe they met each other tonight. The woman presses the number twenty-two and the man starts to kiss me once we get to floor ten, press me up against the mirrored elevator walls, while she just watches and plays with her hair. As if we're a boring movie.

I kiss him back eventually. His tongue tastes like burnt orange and alcohol, and I know I'm not going to be able to come when I have sex with him, his taste is all wrong. That happens to me if the person doesn't smell or taste right.

He pulls on my hand and takes me down the hall to his apartment and unlocks the door, his girlfriend trailing after us. She keeps trying to catch my eye, keeps trying to smile at me with that mouth, but I have to look away. The cold blue of her eyes hurts me for some reason.

A clean beige couch in the living room faces a brand-new TV. The balcony hangs over the city, slowly being covered in snow. Burying any traces that might remain of Jenade. Even all these years later I feel there must be something left. I flick on a lamp on the dining room table, and it glows only faintly, soft orange. "What's wrong with your lamp?" I ask. "Mood lighting?"

"It's a sun lamp," he tells me. He wants to get me back close to him. His arms reach for me, but I'm exploring the apartment.

"Is that for SAD?"

"It's to mimic a sunrise," he says, and the light grows with brightness until the whole room's lit.

The woman laughs. "Some sunrise," she says, and I think about the smile in her voice after she swallowed her tequila.

"Come on," he says, and grabs my hand again, dragging me along to the bedroom.

The smell of his taste is in the bedroom. The sweetness. The woman touches my shoulder, and I shrug her off, still not able to look at her. He's kissing me again, pressing his crotch against mine, unbuttoning my pants. But I push away his hand. My body isn't mine, it can't remember the Jill from earlier, trolling for someone to take her home.

Jenade's finger. A shin with an exposed bone. A few strands of her thick dark hair.

I step away from the couple, put the bed between them and me.

"What the hell?" the man says.

An arm here, a leg there.

"Just give me a minute," I say, and walk around his room. "Not everything can always happen so fast." I turn on another lamp, and its light also swells slowly. I can't even see his face, and I know she's come up behind me. I can feel her heat, making my skin tingle all over.

"Well, fuck," he says, and goes into the bathroom, slamming the door.

His girlfriend apologizes, putting her hand on my arm, telling me so many things, not able to stop talking. I grab my purse and slip out, and she comes with me, easing the door closed so it doesn't make a sound.

Dani, 2010

What do you think of Chris?

Jenade says she doesn't think it's fair that we still talk, she misses you. She was there for you with Alex, so she doesn't understand why, with Chris, everything is different... Okay, yeah, we can just watch another episode. Let me get the DVD.

Are you still there? Good. Okay, are you ready? Press Play. Awesome.

So, how do you like your classes? Come on, just pause it. We never get to talk and it took me three different convenience stores to find a calling card. It'd be nice if we could just chat for a minute instead of watching a show.

I'm really happy here. Like I can't even believe it. Carol's doing all this amazing work in sexology, and it's totally giving my marks a boost. And the reading is actually interesting. Like there's this one study I read about hypersexuality in older women, and there's this woman who is like eighty, but still likes to have sex tons of times a day. One day that will be us. It makes me feel good, like it doesn't even matter with age or anything, we can just keep on going. Carol totally gets my sexuality. We try, like, everything. You'd love to see what we do with toys, Jill. I mean, I know you wouldn't be into seeing, I know you're not really into watching, you prefer to be watched, right?

Anyway, I visited Mom over the break and went through my old closet and guess what I found? One of your old plays! God, it was gross. I loved it. I've started to write too! Carol and

I are going to write a book on kink and sell it in her shop, maybe even find a publisher, isn't that cool? Jill? Are you still there?

Jill, 2009

Sometimes I bring my laptop into a lecture hall to talk to Jenade on MSN or I send her long rambling emails about the other people in the class or the professor or write her plays or little stories like when we were in high school. Some are erotic, but some just are about people and their lives and what they would eventually do or terrible things they've done. I wrote her one long confession about Alex, about how it wasn't even that I'd necessarily wanted to cheat on him; I'd wanted to erase him. It's the only writing I've been doing.

Chris knows about the messages between us. He's seen them. Jenade told me about it. She laughed, lying on her back on my bed, her feet up and pressing against my wall. "He read your last email and he said, 'Man, what a creep.'"

"Oh my god, you didn't show him, did you?"

"Nah, he went into my account."

"Seriously? He went into your email."

"Yeah, it's pretty annoying. He's been figuring out my passwords and going into my email, my phone. It's like a game to him. But he gets pissed when I change the passwords, like I'm hiding something."

"What would you be hiding?"

"Emails from my creepy friends!"

"Fuck that, I'm not a creep, I'm a perv."

"It's the same thing," Jenade said, dancing one foot across the wall to meet her other one and then dancing it back away.

"No, it's not. Like, there's something menacing about a creep."

"But I think there's something like that about a perv too."

"About all of us?"

Jenade bent her head back and smiled at me. I was standing behind the bed and came and put my hands into her hair and pushed it off her forehead. She closed her eyes and felt my hands pass over her and breathed out slowly and peacefully.

She reached and grabbed my hand where it was still slicking back her hair and pulled me down onto the bed beside her.

Jill, 2010

They publish Chris's face in all the newspapers. Turns out he's the creep, not me. I go home to be with family. I study for finals but know I won't finish. My parents immediately put the papers into this wicker basket they keep for recycling, wondering why I'm not crying or breaking down, which I never do, I never have, not with Alex, not about Jenade or anything else that ever happened to me. I dig through the basket of papers and pull them out and spread them across the floor after my parents go to sleep. A graduation photo of Jenade beside a mug shot of Chris. It doesn't seem fair. Aside from the orange jumpsuit, Chris still looks like Chris, and Jenade will never look like Jenade again.

The Woman with the Mouth, December 2013

I'm sorry he upset you. I thought you'd want a guy there, I could tell you wanted me, but you seemed scared. I thought you'd want it with him. But we can go somewhere, just the two of us. I just wanted you, you know. You're so lovely. I want to make you feel good. I'll come with you, wherever you're going. It can just be us.

Alex, December 2013

Hello? Jill?
Are you okay?
I can't understand you.
I'm busy right now, I can't really talk.
Are you safe? How much have you had to drink?

Jill?

Are you still there?

I'm sorry, Jill, I can't hear you.

Jill, 2010

And there was that one night when I received six missed calls from Jenade. I watched each one appear on my screen, and each one reminded me of what it felt like when I'd cheated on Alex. That it wasn't really something I could control. How I'd just gotten drunk at a bar and asked a man to take me home, the way I still did now. "Just walk with me," I'd said, and then I was bending over a chair I had jammed against the wall between my bed and my closet. I always lived in places too small for my things. The man had been oddly sweet with me. "Is this okay?" he'd asked as he thrust into me. He'd guide me into a new position and I kept my eyes blank and I was so drunk. "Are you sure you haven't had too much to drink?" Maybe he didn't ask me that during, maybe that was before, or when we met up a second time, or when I called him telling him I'd drive to see him after I told Alex I was leaving him and never wanted to see him again. That guy's sweet voice made me sick, it was just like Alex's. I wanted the harsh blue eyes of Penny, I wanted the silent, watchful presence of Dani, I wanted the idealism of Jenade most of all. I wanted her body curled up beside me, mine. Her name popped up again and again on my phone's screen that night, and I had the harsh eyes of Penny and the voyeuristic fascination of Dani, but could never be idealistic with that pit in my chest. How many times would she call me? When she stopped at six, I felt cheated. It was as if she barely wanted to talk to me at all.

CAMERA

Phone cameras can be hacked, all the photos uploaded to cyberspace. But the hot-pink Fuji camera, the one her mom gave her, has been shoved into the back of a desk drawer and has a cracked screen and she's lost the chargers for her other small cameras. She has a rental from school kicking around beside her bed, where anyone could step on it, but she doesn't want this mixed up with that. Something about using her phone's camera is more intimate, purer. Almost as if he's just in the room watching her. She has to film it fresh. In the past, she's used masking tape to secure her phone to a mug. Today she props the phone against books, uses a couple of novels to pin the front so it doesn't slide down as she's filming. She lies on her bed, reclines. She sees a text from him drop down at the top of the screen. *Hellllllloooooo. Hurrrryyyy uppppp.* She inserts two fingers inside herself. She doesn't worry about making it look like porn. She just wants to be naked and feel good and be real. She doesn't make herself come. She knows her fingers are probably blocking his view of her lips, how wet she is. Her palm grinds into her clit as her index and middle fingers search for her G-spot. When it feels good, she makes noises unique to her body. Then she turns off the camera.

When she was nineteen, her first boyfriend positioned the Fuji camera to capture her tits. Even though kids send each other snaps of their junk before they even graduate middle school now, back then she could barely believe what she was doing. Felt braver than all of her friends. Felt dirtier.

In front of the camera held by her first boyfriend, she stopped being shy. She stopped caring what anyone would ever think of her, what he thought of her. Right before they had sex, she always knew that she was wonderful, that all of her was made to be adored. The Fuji camera pressed in his hand as he laughed shyly, his penis hard and standing in front of him, pointing slightly to the right the way it always did.

She'd never thought of herself as someone who sheds people, but she shed him and kept the camera, kept the files saved deeply in her computer. One folder said Work Stuff, then the one inside said Fish, and then the one inside said Cookies, and that's where they were. This was so her parents wouldn't stumble across them if they ever used her computer. She still lived at home at the time. She wondered if he had saved them too but didn't care too much. A video of them having sex together in which you couldn't see penis going into vagina, couldn't see anything, could hear only the soft sounds of two people in love who are learning to have sex, exploring. Still too shy with each other and sex to even talk dirty. It would give him nothing, and they give her nothing now, but she enjoys knowing she made them, enjoys knowing they exist.

No matter what anyone tells you, a naked body is lovely. When her lovers are sprawled in the dim light of her bedroom, one leg extended and the other bent, their backs supported by a mound of pillows and their penises gently resting against one leg, she begs them to let her take their pictures. Each picture she dreams of painting in many colours and then hanging up on her wall. Even parts of the body that most people agree are ugly—the scrotum, the taint, a hairy asshole—become the parts of her lovers that she wants to lick and bite, to have rubbed all over her.

Nothing can be wrong with a body, she thinks, and each body she sees, small, crooked, wounded, or large, is attractive—in fact, if she is being honest, she has always thought there is something attractive about a tall, hairy, huge man she can climb. She fantasizes about big breasts pressing into her face, although she hasn't had much experience with women. Eventually, she tells herself some days, and then other days she forgets about it altogether. Too shy or too distracted. And it isn't just women with large butts and breasts that make her excited. Almost anyone catches her interest. A woman who is thin and pulled inward, a mouth that has a constantly bitten bottom lip. Someone small, boyish, with closely clipped hair. "See me naked," she wants to say. "Let's take a bath together." She watches these people on the subway. The way they sit. The angle of their shoulders. When she falls in love, most of the time, it is about the way a person talks, but this isn't about talking, or the expressions a person makes when they listen to you or how they laugh or what they think about death, if they can offer you comfort on your hardest days; this is about raw attraction, and bodies, all the sexy bodies.

Even before her first boyfriend, she knew. In Grade 4, she cried, hiding in the alcove beside the school doors, because the boy she loved was mean to her again for no reason. She cried and couldn't stop. Why couldn't he understand that she needed no one to ever be mean to her, she needed people who would tell her things that she'd never noticed about herself and to put an extra coat around her so she could exist with bravery and strength. A girl in her class whom she hated—and of course that hate made much more sense now that she was older—bent over to comfort her and her shirt hung down and a bit of lace decorated her concave, still-childlike chest, the edge of a bra. She thought she'd never be able to breathe again. She definitely stopped crying, as the girl rubbed her shoulder and she tried to keep her eyes from drifting toward the white lace, the hint of what would be there eventually.

A thirst for all bodies, women, men, non-binary, cis or trans, and definitely of any race or culture—that's what she has. *Is there anyone I'm not attracted to?* she wonders. *Any type?* Certain people who are too controlled, too polished, make her feel nervous, but maybe that nervousness would also be able to flip inside out to attraction in the right circumstances. Maybe, if she's honest, she's a person who wants all of it.

This is why it makes sense to share her body.

She sends him the video, and she knows he'll understand it. That he'll like it. Because he'll get that it's real. *You're so hot*, he texts back.

Send me something, she asks.

I can't, he says. *But next time, I'll film you.*

When they finally meet up to have sex, he takes out his phone and films his dick pushing into her pussy. They are doing it doggy style, and so in the frame, you can see her ass and his dick. He sends it to her so she has a copy, and then they watch the video together and have sex again, with her lying chest-down on the bed and him lying on top of her. She picks up her phone after, points at him.

"Stop it," he says, and ducks out of her view. She does it again and this time he grabs for her phone. "I told you I don't like it. Why do you have to be a child?"

She walks home from his place in North York, past strip malls and skinny trees pinned to iron railings, with the video of them having sex in her pocket. Why only her, not him? It should be easier to be content. She has a video of herself she's filmed for him, shared with him. She has a video of them having sex together, even though you can only see his dick. But it's not enough.

When he grabbed at her phone, she wanted to tell him it was because he was beautiful and he looked so different from what he looked like with his clothes on. In a way, men's clothes are much more about keeping body parts hidden. When she wears clothes, you can't see her nipples or her vagina, but her shirts hug her bras, which hug her breasts. Her pants cling to her skin as tightly as possible. Most of the girls in her college classes dress like this. The boys in her classes tend to wear sweats, and you can't see anything. You can't even see the shape of their legs. Boys and men sometimes send her and her friends their dicks when they don't want to see them. They all talk about it. How sending dick pics is gross because it lacks context. And not only the context of a request but also the context of the sender. Just a floating part, hiding the rest of them, the rest of their skin hidden away as if they're ashamed to be alive. She thinks most men she knows are ashamed in this way.

During their class on Monday, he won't look at her. He goes so far as to sit with another group. The teacher is too bored to notice. Storyboards today. She is uninterested because it isn't real. She leaves when her classes switch. She'll only do one more semester, if that.

She's enrolled in film and television because she wanted to learn about production. But without sex, she finds her film and television courses mundane. Who cares about a commercial? Who cares about the way the lens frames a scene? It means nothing, isn't saying anything. She spends most of her class time drawing in the margins of her notebook. Cartoons with bulging eyes and drooling mouths. Sharp, pointed teeth.

"Why do you always act like you don't care?" he asked her once during a group project, frustrated by her lack of motivation.

When a sex video or naked pictures get leaked, everyone freaks out. She doesn't understand this. Isn't that the you who isn't filtered by clothes or money or the people you spend time with? All people are naked sometimes. She knows some people are more protective of their bodies, feel the need to protect their bodies, but who cares about the colour of your nipples or the length of your labia, how much hair you have, if your dick is short and fat or long and thin or curved as if it's asking a question? Who cares.

The day he joins another group in class isn't the end. One late night, they meet up again. He pretends to want only sex, but she knows he likes talking to her. She thinks maybe she could fall in love with him. He lies on his bed in his bachelor apartment and she fills a glass of water at the sink. She drinks it down all at once while he talks. About how he wants to be a great director and that maybe he'll work in the industry for a bit and gain experience once their program is done, and if he really needs to, he'd be open to going back to school, to university; his college grades are good enough. He's top of all his classes. "What about you?" he asks her.

She flips through the videos on her phone, not looking at him. Videos she's taken both for him and others and for herself. In one, she reads naked for thirty minutes in a big, plush, green chair her parents gave her when she moved out. She's always liked books even though she's a lousy student.

"Hello?" he says. "Sometimes it's like you don't listen to me."

"I am," she says. "I do. All I do is listen to you."

"What's that supposed to mean?"

When they have sex that night and the next few times, they don't use their phones to take any videos. She's afraid to bring it up until she's drunk.

"I know why you won't let me film you," she says. "It's all

about control, right?" She thinks of him behind the camera, him in class, him with his future plans, plans to be great one day. And great how? Wanting people to walk around and say great, great, great. What a genius. She realizes that when he films her, he thinks it's about submission. She stops returning his texts. She acts as if he isn't even in class, when she goes.

He will, of course, do well in the film industry. He'll begin with production roles and maybe one day he'll direct. He will stay up all night if he has to, he'll never fall in love if he has to. He'll never be caught doing anything that would ruin his image, although she'll still get a text from him from time to time, a floating dick out of context, words asking her, *Happy now?* And she'll always delete them.

While she's in the college cafeteria inserting a bagel into the toaster, spreading butter and then spreading jam, she forgets who she is for a minute and where she is. It's like being on drugs or being lost in a nightmare. It's like being in front of the camera, and her hand instantly slips into her pocket, touches the side of her phone.

A woman beside her with short dark hair reaches over her to grab a sesame bagel from the rack. As the dark-haired woman puts the bagel into the slicer, the edge of her hand slips against hers. She apologizes, smiles. For a minute, the girl hesitates. She thinks that maybe her videos have leaked after all and that's why the dark-haired woman is looking at her this way. But then she smiles back.

Isn't it disgusting?

TWO SEX ADDICTS
FALL IN LOVE

A sex addict meets another sex addict and falls in love.

Sex Addict 1 needs sex all the time, but it can be with the same person as long as

1. It's interesting
2. The person smells good
3. They both come at least once almost every time
4. It is done in many new ways with a sense of adventure.

Sex Addict 1 knows she loves Sex Addict 2, forever and ever.

Sex Addict 2 needs sex all the time, but hopefully

1. With as many people as possible
2. In as many different ways as possible
3. In unexpected circumstances
4. Without needing to worry about anyone's feelings.

Sex Addict 2 cares about Sex Addict 1's feelings but is constantly thinking about the lists. Sex Addict 2 also isn't sure he believes in love—he's never seen it, at least, despite the bond he feels with Sex Addict 1. Also, how can love exist when the lists exist?

When sex addicts dream of the perfect person to love them, they dream of a sex addict. And at first it *is* perfect. Sex Addict 2 finally feels that lying does not have to be part of his addiction, that he can have sex regularly with someone he cares about and still be able to nurture his urges and have someone who will try new things, explore his fantasies, and understand his needs. Sex Addict 1 feels that sexual compatibility is probably the way to true intimacy and that if she finally has someone she finds attractive, interesting, good-smelling, and funny to have sex with multiple times a day, then they must be soulmates.

At first, Sex Addict 2 seems to agree. One night when they are out for dinner, Sex Addict 1 congratulates Sex Addict 2 on how decent he is when they disagree—that he never yells or swears at her or even seems to get too angry. Usually, if he becomes angry or upset, he'll verbalize his feelings instead. "I'm feeling angry," he'll say. "I'm hurt by what you said." Or sometimes he'll even break down his feelings further: "I'm not angry with you. I'm just annoyed. I'm frustrated." Coming from a family of yelling and cursing and emotions that never seemed to be resolved, Sex Addict 1 finds this trait endearing in Sex Addict 2. Sex Addict 2 says, "Well, I don't know what we'd really have to fight about. We seem to agree on everything."

That night they get into a fight. It is a version of the same fight they will continue to have and that previously was a "discussion" about the fate of their relationship. Each fight comes closer to the inevitable truth: they have different items on their lists. Somehow, in deciding they are perfect for each other, Sex Addict 1 and Sex Addict 2 have fallen back into their old patterns and have been lying.

In fact, if Sex Addict 1 is honest, it isn't sex that draws her in, or even the intimacy—it's feeling as if her whole body is being erased, that she's surrounded. She needs to be hugged, she needs to be held, she needs to be enveloped, she needs to smell parts of another human's body. She might not even be a sex addict at all—sometimes it's easy for her to think about other things, to let ideas be what hold her, envelop her. Sometimes she dances around the kitchen and that feels almost as good. But if her connection with Sex Addict 2 finds its basis in their mutual sex addiction, then she can never renounce her identity as a sex addict or even be more specific about what it actually is.

It is unclear if the situation Sex Addict 1 and 2 find themselves in can be framed as being "A sex addict meets another sex addict and falls in love." If Sex Addict 2 doubts the very existence of love (or at least his own ability to love actively in a way that makes them both feel good), then perhaps he has never allowed himself to exist in the state of "being in love," or if he has, he has not allowed himself to recognize this state as being in love, or allowed himself to exist within that state for any real amount of time before rushing off to pursue his addiction.

If Sex Addict 2 has never "been in love" with Sex Addict 1, then it is doubtful that Sex Addict 1 has ever "been in love" with Sex Addict 2. Sex Addict 1 tries to figure this situation out with her friends the way she tries to figure everything out—by speaking. She tells them about the lists. She describes the different positions she and Sex Addict 2 have done. She describes her fear of being alone and her desire to be completely encased. She gives examples of Sex Addict 2's behaviour and asks for interpretation. She gets almost the same answer, just with different diction, depending on the friend: "He doesn't seem to be a very self-aware person. Whereas you seem to be! I'm amazed by your awareness." Sex Addict 1 appreciates compliments during times like this, although from the details provided about Sex Addicts 1 and 2, this assessment can be understood to be false.

Sex Addict 1 has not selected her friends according to the trend of picking people whom you admire professionally or want to be in some capacity, who dedicate their conversational power to the discussion of their ambitions and interests and reveal very little of their interpersonal lives. Sex Addict 1, while admiring her friends for their talents and abilities, has chosen her friends for their compassion, creativity, and what she (as much as she can tell, being a poor judge of character) thinks are their good hearts. She enjoys the long hours they spend tolerating her as she talks about herself, love, and sex. But since these people are fully developed, they would also enjoy speaking about

1. Their interests
2. Outer space
3. Animals
4. The existence of ghosts
5. New scientific discoveries
6. The upcoming election
7. Pipelines
8. A new position they may get
9. A movie they just saw
10. Their families
11. The war in Syria
12. Their health
13. A plane that went missing
14. An upcoming event that they have to go to but really don't want to go to
15. Netflix

and get frustrated by the limited nature of Sex Addict 1's focus. On some level, Sex Addict 1 also acknowledges that the crumbling partnership between her and Sex Addict 2 was always fairly shallow. "It's only about attraction and pain. Why did I ever think those things are deep? They aren't about the world, they aren't about goals, dreams, secret desires, they aren't about life or death. They aren't even about the person, not really." Her friends nod along and try to change the subject. Sex Addict 1 has exhausted her lines of support.

It's hard to say what will become of Sex Addict 2. Some of their mutual friends say they see him going for walks around the city. Some say he's learning how to be on his own. Some say he thinks about love sometimes, wonders if he's wrong, thinks maybe he can do it. He's always been surprised by the way time moves around him, and maybe it's a new season now—it's getting colder. He blows on his hands and pushes them deeper into his pockets.

The world is also changing around Sex Addict 1. Perhaps this is because she is no longer seeing everything through the lens of sex. She always thought she was a pretty decent human being except when it came to sex, and then sometimes she did things she didn't quite mean to do. For instance, when she first met Sex Addict 2, after some mild flirting, she informed him that he was in love with her and then tried to grab his dick through his pants underneath the table, even though they were at a bar surrounded by people, even though he had a girlfriend at the time. Sex Addict 1 had also been drinking, which of course didn't help any of that behaviour, but feeling sexual like that felt like being drunk anyway, somehow uninhibited, somehow operating on pure instinct.

Whenever Sex Addict 1 thinks about this behaviour in isolation, she thinks that this behaviour must belong to a bad person, that it's the addiction, but then when she turns it around and looks at it another way, it seems as if most every person is like that, sometimes at least. Other times, it's as if she's separate from herself in those moments and there is a real split in herself and the her who needs sex is there to destroy the her who needs tenderness, the her who needs to be shielded, hugged, cared for. Sex Addict 1 has never understood why she can't occupy both these spaces at once and thinks something must be wrong with her.

In the early morning, Sex Addict 1 goes for a run. She is trying to replace a hunger for sex with taking care of herself. Sometimes when she misses Sex Addict 2, she uses a vibrator. These sessions can last hours, but somehow in these moments of masturbation, Sex Addict 1 finds that she's able to merge sex with tenderness, or at least blur the lines slightly. Not that she tries to fantasize about tenderness, but she recognizes that the very act of pleasuring herself in this way is an act of tenderness, especially if it means she's not opening herself up to Sex Addict 2 again. As she runs in the morning, she feels the same thing—the borders of her physicality break up so that the heart that has always been a little too sore in her is released and beating and her brain is quiet and sun is staining the sky all over in pink and purple and orange.

TIGHT 'N' BRIGHT (THE LOWEST POINT IN MY LIFE)

Sometimes I wake up in the middle of the night, from one bad dream or another. I get up, eat a banana, drink a glass of water, maybe make a cup of peppermint tea. I play so many pieces of my life back like snippets—remember confessing to my best friend, Sam, that I felt as though I wanted to die and that she was the only one I could tell at that time. The lowest point in my life plays over in my head, so many bad relationships and unrequited loves, when after enough time it became clear that it was all me: I was the one drinking too much and throwing fits, hurting people's feelings and acting the fool, all because I hoped to be found interesting.

Alone in my apartment, I find this pathetic. I know, in theory, that I should treat my past self with compassion, recognize her for being the young person she was, but god, I hate her.

That's when I think of calling Sam. I'll tell her I need her, that I've never had a friend like her, and ask her why she's drifted from me. Then I realize that this overdramatization of a very simple thing—missing an intense friendship—is exactly what always went wrong, that I am tired and more prone to worrying in the middle of the night, that I'm not myself, and should put myself back to sleep.

I was twenty-three and Sam was twenty-four. Or maybe I was twenty-four and Sam was twenty-five. Either way, we didn't have the fear yet, and we lived each day that summer as if we'd never die. Not that many bad things had happened to us yet, I hadn't quit drinking, and everything was exciting. We were going to take a cab down to the harbour at Yonge and Front and go on a daytime cruise. Sam was great at partying. She went to many boat parties, but usually they lasted a whole night until the morning was coming, and then kept going even longer. The ones during the middle of the day were for people who weren't true partiers: bros and their girlfriends, people who partied for pictures on social media. But Sam's friend's boyfriend was DJing and she was loyal and wanted to support him. We also wanted to drink.

The only catch was that this party had the theme of Tight 'n' Bright. Which basically meant you needed to wear something that was tight and bright. I'd picked out a magenta lace tube dress, which was too formal, too hot, too dark, but at the time I thought it made me exceptionally attractive. It did not. But Sam swore I looked great, as she tried to decide what to wear herself. She finally pulled on a bright tank top and black skirt. Her belt was thick and black and her eye makeup was almost goth. "Fuck Tight 'n' Bright," she said. "No boat is telling me what to wear."

As the cab approached the boat, we saw herds of bros in pink and yellow neon tanks, girls walking in neon swimwear and crop tops, bright white shorts and skirts. As soon as we got on, people threw Mardi Gras beads over our necks in blue and purple and gold. The whole boat looked as if some little kid had eaten a box of crayons and then either shit or puked it out. I was disgusted with myself for being there, but then Sam put her arm around my waist and gave me a hug, saying, "Kylie, I love you." I felt as if I'd give up every good thing in my life for a friend like Sam.

The sun was hot, and it probably was only just creeping up to 1:00 p.m., and I was soon drunk on Corona. I'd forgotten I hate boats. They rock and make you sick, and they only ever sell one type of beer. My mouth tasted like old bread and lime. The alcohol made me lonely, although I was dancing with Sam and her friend, right by where the boyfriend DJ'd.

I started looking for a love. A cameraman was videoing the whole thing for the production company that ran the boat. He was a type I often was into—skinny and troubled, out of place on the cruise, like me. I kept trying to goad him into having a real conversation, one that acknowledged that we both didn't know how we'd ended up on a day cruise like this, that we didn't actually know how we'd come to know the people we knew, that our thoughts were so much deeper than those of the people around us.

Despite all this, he didn't really notice me. Girls were everywhere, all tighter and brighter than me. He filmed people he felt were interesting, and I followed him, dancing as close as I could without blocking him. He turned his camera to a man who was tall, shirtless, broad-chested, and grinning. That smile—I was in love already. He had the whitest smile I'd ever seen, the perfect shape, like all the movie stars have, a crescent moon fallen to rest on the face of a man. He was obviously a bro, not my usual type, and I had no desire to talk to him. I just wanted to have sex with him—then and there. I joined a group of girls who all seemed to know him and danced on the outskirts of the circle, hoping he'd notice me, the cameraman forgotten.

And he did notice me. He gave me the elevator and I thought he was checking out my tits, but then I realized he was checking out my dark magenta dress. "Hi," I said with a huge smile, and took a swig from my beer bottle. "Sorry, this not tight or bright enough for you?"

"This is my brother," he said, and gestured to a guy beside him. A kid, really. The brother had the same smile, but his face was fleshier. He was wearing a neon green tank top that looked as if it'd been washed with something brown. This was Tight 'n'

Bright. The boy from the lowest point of my life.

"How old are you anyway?" I asked.

"Twenty-one," he said.

"Aw, that's not that bad then." He glared at me and told me I looked barely nineteen. I told him my actual age and then began to tell him about my adventure with Sam to the bathroom. We'd stumbled across a group of boys near the front of the boat when we were looking for the bathroom and some fresh air. They were all holding on to each other and howling into the sky, directly at the sun, "Coke! Coke! I need some coke! Do you know where I can find some coke?" One ran right up to me, giggling. "Know anyone on this damn boat with some coke, sweetheart?"

Back then, Sam only did drugs that made her dance, and wasn't old and weary enough to need drugs to wake her up. By the time I was thirty, I understood why everyone tried the drugs they did, even though I never dabbled in anything other than weed. Drugs weren't something that caused people to be evil or always originated from a self-destructive impulse, the way my binge drinking did. A lot of the time, people did drugs out of sheer self-preservation, trying to get through another night or find enjoyment in things. Then bad luck or genetics or lack of foresight got some people hooked. That was all.

At the time, though, I feared drugs and the people who did them, as if those people belonged to another world that teetered at the edge of mine and, if I let them, they would consume me. I knew I wanted to rip myself apart, and allowing access to anything that would make me go insane quicker than I already was going on my own was dangerous. So I told Tight 'n' Bright, "I don't like that stuff, do you?"

"Nah, I'm not into that," he said. He seemed, momentarily, willing to connect with me. "My brother is, some of his friends, but I'm just not into it." I wonder if that's still true of Tight 'n' Bright, or if it was just because he hadn't grown up yet.

We stopped talking because it was getting us nowhere and began to dance to the music. He bought us more beers and I drank mine quickly. "You're done already? I'm not buying you another," he said.

"Do you have somewhere we can go after?"

"Yeah. We can go to my brother's place," he said.

Earlier that summer, Sam and her boyfriend broke up, so we hit up the LCBO. She grabbed a two-litre bottle of wine off the shelf. We got a small bottle of vodka and some juice for us to drink at her sublet. "What's the wine for?" I asked. "Going to a party?"

"It's for my depression," she said. She was only half joking, I knew. Sam had moved into a sweltering sublet, a condo like a box, with no AC. She spent most of that summer drunk and sweating, which is what people tend to do, at least in Toronto, when they're going through a breakup during the summer, when everyone expects you to be outside and happy, smiling into the sun like we-can't-believe-winter's-over. *Of course* Sam had to drink. She was always ready to meet up, so we could go on another adventure or just complain about our lives or run errands together.

At her place, we got so drunk I could barely walk. I think that was the night we went to a party for Pride, but I can't remember. I found some shirtless guy and we made out while people danced around us. "Trust you to find some guy to make out with at Pride," she said.

I laughed and shrugged. In my mind, almost everyone was bisexual anyway. I certainly was.

I fell asleep on Sam's floor inside a duvet and woke up sweating with a pounding headache. She was right, the apartment did hold in the heat. I got up. "Sam," I said. She didn't move. I was too hungover to even know what to do. I needed to get home to my cool basement apartment, curl up, and fall asleep until my headache left me.

Her eyes sprung open. She turned and looked at me.

"Hi," I said.

"Holy shit!" She jumped up and pulled her blanket around her, so that only her head poked out. "Kylie, I forgot you were even here."

"I gotta go. My head. I can't."

She was back asleep within minutes. I walked home, even though it took about an hour. I couldn't really afford a cab or even transit. Even in a heat wave, it was cooler outside than in her apartment. I wondered why I'd drunk so much, why I'd made out with that guy, why Sam was scared when she saw me in her apartment, who I really was. I began to cry as I walked home. I didn't know if it was because of the pain in my head, my life, or what. Even though I was poor, I was luckier than most, I knew. I had an education, I had Sam, I had a family I could call on the phone and confide in. Maybe that's when the hate in me started to grow. But I've told you before, it's always been there, always.

Tight 'n' Bright grabbed my hand, and we walked away from the harbour and across the parking lot. Someone was puking beside a car, while their friends filmed it on a smart phone. All of the pink-neon-clad cruisegoers found their cars or walked up toward the street to take cabs home. None of the boat people took streetcars. I'm sure they felt like public transit was beneath them. They were just that kind of people—not like me and Sam. By this point, I'd lost Sam and sent her a text to tell her where I was going. I knew she'd come looking for me if I disappeared or ended up dead.

"Are we going to get more booze?" I asked him. "I don't have anything to drink."

He flashed me a credit card that his brother had given

him, pointed out an LCBO. He tugged my hand, dragging me toward the store. Inside, I let go of him, weaved in and out of the aisles. I still felt like I had as a kid, going in there with my parents, asking questions about the different-coloured bottles, trying to get my mom to buy ones that had pictures on them. Pretending I was of age, standing in line with six bottles of wine while my mother ran to get one she'd forgotten. I had one of those moments with Tight 'n' Bright too, where I worried that I'd lost him like a kid loses a parent in a supermarket, that I'd be left in the store until some other adult chose to bring me home. I found him with a small bottle of vodka in his hand.

"This is for my brother," he said.

"That's not enough for all of us," I said. I grabbed two tallboys from a display. "Can you buy me these?"

"No."

"No?"

"It's my brother's card. I'm not buying you shit."

"I thought you liked me."

"You'll have to buy your own."

We waited side by side in line. I used my credit card to buy the two tallboys. I was furious. I'm not sure why I felt he should buy my beer for me. I was worried about money all the time, and I guess I thought that if he wanted me to stay out and go to his brother's with him, at least he'd buy me a drink.

We argued all the way to his brother's lakeshore condo. The sun was finally starting to set behind a row of skyscrapers, the light sharp and violent in its reflections off the glass corners. Going up into those buildings would have been impossible to me, even just a few hours ago. No one there wanted me.

Sam moved up north with her first husband when we were in our late twenties, and we lost touch for a bit. At the beginning, I'd call her. She'd say, "Thank fuck you called—I've been going crazy here all by myself with just Travis." He liked to hunt, would go on trips for days at a time. It seemed as if mostly she just did drugs. She had a job teaching at a school just outside a reserve. Sometimes she'd cry to me about all the problems the kids had—she cared so much and was broken when she couldn't do anything to help. My phone would go off in the middle of the night and it would be Sam, ranting about her life, how cold it was up there in winter, how she thought Travis was fucking around. She had a knack for always calling while I was masturbating. Sometimes I'd finish and call her back; other times, I just wiped my hand and answered her call, slightly out of breath. She never noticed.

I quit drinking because it was making my life horrible. It wasn't that I had a problem—at least that's what I told myself. I just was sick of feeling like a shit-show. I found that after I quit drinking, it was easier to hold the rest of my life together. Easier to realize I had very few close friends and that was something I could change. I saw a therapist and we used phrases like "incremental change" and "positive action." I was beginning to live a life that didn't make me want to kill myself. Tight 'n' Bright began to seem like one rough episode in a life that would be long, peaceful, and happy. The me who'd experienced Tight 'n' Bright still existed, but she was tired and pleased with herself for making decisions more slowly and for finding time to be alone. For realizing that true love wasn't found in a bar or on a boat. I still didn't know where true love was, but I felt more confident that it existed and that I'd find something good for me one day.

At Tight 'n' Bright's brother's condo, I tried talking to people, but they turned to each other instead as I sipped one whole tallboy down and then the other. Everyone talked about drugs, getting fucked up. How much drugs cost and the way they made them feel, how much they had and how long they'd last. I whispered to Tight 'n' Bright, "I told you I don't like that stuff."

He said, "Come on," and led me away from these people who didn't like me. It was the only nice thing Tight 'n' Bright ever did for me.

We went into the bathroom. We began to make out sloppily, like teens first learning. I pointed at the shower. "I like water," I said to him. "It makes me horny." He ran the water in the shower and we piled into the bathtub for a second or two with our clothes on, me on top, making out with water streaming down our faces, and then he had his dick out, the skin all soft and wrinkly, and I pulled my panties off and we had sex for a minute without him fully hard before I remembered I wasn't on the pill and we'd better be careful if I didn't want to have Tight 'n' Bright's kid. "Listen, we need a condom," I said, or I just got sick of just rubbing against his semi-hard dick in the bathtub, so he took me to his brother's bedroom.

He kept trying to have sex without a condom, and I kept stopping him, saying, "I'm not on the pill y'know!" with a tone of voice designed to inspire shame. He rooted around underneath his brother's bed. The bed was a king and the bedding was in layers, like you'd see in a hotel—first soft red sheets and then a grey duvet. Pillows in red pillowcases for sleeping and grey pillows for decoration. I thought about his brother's perfect smile, the same smile as Tight 'n' Bright's, but in a better face. Like the room, the box Tight 'n' Bright finally found was made of pristine polished wood. Inside was a folded-up set of condoms.

I couldn't imagine someone lived like Tight 'n' Bright's brother did. It didn't make sense to me. Although I wasn't that much younger than Tight 'n' Bright's brother, I lived in a basement apartment with very little light. I had a double bed that I'd bought when I was eighteen, when I first moved out of my parents' house. Sometimes when I was too lazy to walk to the laundromat, I left the stained mattress bare and slept on it like that. I had long ago broken my bedside table lamp, so it didn't have a shade. I'd tried to duct-tape a shade in place for a while, and some duct tape was still on the lamp, right where you screwed in the light bulb. One night, I'd spilled a glass of water all over the floor and over my lamp and power bar and then touched the water and electrocuted myself. I called my parents crying in the middle of night, worrying that perhaps I would die of delayed heart failure from being electrocuted. I didn't even have a burn.

We kept trying to get a condom on Tight 'n' Bright, but it kept slipping off. He didn't even seem all that concerned with actually getting his dick in me. Instead he started to fingerbang me. It was as brutal as you might imagine. He jammed his fingers in straight, obviously not knowing anything about where the G-spot was (and to be honest, at that time, I didn't really know where it was either), and rammed his fingers in and out faster and faster until I was screaming, "Stop! Stop!" I finally bent my leg up and used my foot to push on his arm at the elbow, pulling his fingers down and away from me. I rolled over onto my stomach.

This would have been a good point to just go home, but something got into me back in those days. It was like no matter how embarrassing the situation was, if we just had sex, it would all be better. I'd feel great, for a moment at least, and not even physically. Psychologically. I especially wanted the feeling of someone's body pressing on me. But I didn't know that at the time.

"Are we ever going to have sex?" I said to Tight 'n' Bright. "Where the hell are the condoms?" He smiled at me and tried to put his fingers into me again. "Stop, do you even know what you're doing?" I said.

"I'm a virgin."

"Really? It's your first time? Look, if it's your first time, you don't want it to be like this, you want it to be with someone special." I rolled onto my back and stared at the ceiling. "I was eighteen when I lost it. It wasn't that I didn't want to before, it just was never right… My boyfriend in high school didn't think we loved each other enough, that I didn't love him, and he thought it was important for me to have sex with someone I loved. I guess it was. But I didn't know I didn't love him, you know, until he told me, I just wanted to have sex so bad. But then I met Jonathan, who I dated for four and a half years before I moved to this hellhole, I mean before I moved to Toronto—well, you know what I mean. And we really loved each other, for a while at least. He loved me. And I was so glad I waited, even though it took longer than I'd wanted." Part of me thought about how this scene would look from the outside—that I was so old and wise compared to this boy, experiencing his first time with a woman, not knowing what to do. I'd been wrong to treat his ignorance with frustration, even cruelty. He needed tenderness in this moment.

"You actually think I'm a virgin?" he said.

I didn't know what to believe. We found a condom and had half-hearted sex. It remains some of the worst sex I've ever had.

When we came out of the room, the place was deserted. It wasn't even midnight. "I've gotta go," I said, and kissed him bye and beat it. I went to the elevator, calling Sam on the way. She picked me up in a cab.

"Where the hell have you been?" She handed me my backpack. She was going over to a friend's place with air conditioning and was determined to eat a whole pizza herself.

"Can I have a little?" I asked.

"You can buy a piece," she said.

"I'll wait till I'm home." At home, all I had were a few sad potatoes keeping each other company on an empty fridge shelf. We both knew it. She bought me a slice and the cab took me home. I thought I'd wake up in the morning and, other than my hangover and a vague bad feeling, it'd be like Tight 'n' Bright never happened.

Around the time Sam's marriage fell apart, I stopped drinking for real. Not just levelling off, not just switching from beer to vodka soda, not just a few drinks when I was out. Nothing. At first, she thought this was pretty great. "I've given up on love, and you're giving up on drinking, perfect," she said. "I should drink less too." She'd already said she was going to stop doing drugs now that she wasn't with Travis anymore, but drinking was something different with her. It wasn't an all-or-nothing thing like I'd always experienced it—I kept quitting and starting, making rules and breaking my own rules. I wasn't an alcoholic, I reasoned, I was just concerned, overly nervous. Both my parents were alcoholics and were usually drunk if I called past 8:00 p.m. I wanted a life that was different. For Sam, drinking was like a quiet thrum in the background, sometimes louder and quieter, but always there.

It wasn't long before she stopped calling me. Sometimes we'd still hang out, but it was always in the daytime, when I wouldn't be tempted to drink. I made new friends, I became an active person, sometimes it felt as if I had a totally new personality, especially if I compared myself to the person who'd been with Tight 'n' Bright, but then I'd remember myself as a child, sitting on a hill, feeling the sun, pulling blades of grass from the ground, writing or singing to myself little songs I'd made up. Happiest alone.

When I woke up, I had Tight 'n' Bright's number in my phone and I was missing my sunglasses and my watch. I instantly knew I'd forgotten them at his brother's place. *Lots of people forgot stuff,* he texted me back. *Message my brother, I'm sure he'll help you.* He gave me his brother's number and then we never spoke again.

I went back to the condo by the lake. Found enough coins

to take the subway both ways and rode south for about an hour, thinking about what I'd be walking into. What did his brother think of me—locking myself first in the bathroom and then in the bedroom with his younger brother? Using all the condoms from his stash. Forgetting my belongings somewhere deep in the recesses of the apartment.

I didn't find any sunglasses, his brother had texted me. I was surprised that he used full sentences, apostrophes. *My friend had his wallet stolen too.* The sunglasses had been expensive, a gift from my mother, and I'd managed not to lose them for two years. One boat cruise later and they were gone. *I have your watch though.*

As I rode the elevator up to his place, I worried. That he would kill me, rape me, that I would be found all over the city in pieces, that I would never see Sam or my parents again, that I'd finally made the mistake that meant I'd be gone for good. I also thought about the flipside—what if I got there, and he saw me, and he fell in love with me? He would invite me to live in the condo, and although, on principle, I didn't like condos, I would like living with him very much. In my fantasy, he never wore a shirt and we never left the apartment.

I glanced at myself in the mirrored walls of the elevator and was faced with my own shabbiness. I was not unattractive, but I definitely was a slob, and things like the heat or the rain made me look wild. I also didn't know how to make any of my clothes look as if they belonged together or as if they would even be picked out by the same person. For instance, I was wearing a crummy dress and runners from Walmart that were beginning to wear through. I believed looking put together meant that you bought into capitalism, were shallow, and had no soul. But for a moment, before knocking on the brother's door, I regretted these beliefs.

He invited me in, and I stood in the hallway of his apartment beside a set of golf clubs. "One second," he said the instant he opened the door. He smiled the crescent moon but didn't make eye contact with me.

He walked over to his kitchen counter, grabbed the watch from his grey granite countertop. The band was fraying. If I'd been a different person, it wouldn't even have been worth going back for. I took the watch from him, thanked him. He said it was no problem but looked annoyed. One more ride down the elevator and that would be it, I thought. Enough of Tight 'n' Bright. Enough of these trailing results of Tight 'n' Bright.

I'd like to be able to tell you I learned something from Tight 'n' Bright, from the lowest point in my life, but I can't really say I did. I also don't really know why I considered Tight 'n' Bright the lowest point, when really so many others were still to come. I guess Tight 'n' Bright made me feel humiliated—a piece of shit destined for other pieces of shit—committed to living a life that made me terrified for myself. I knew what I was doing, I knew I needed to lean away from it, but had chosen to lean in. I was aware of myself and my decisions. Perhaps Tight 'n' Bright was really that moment, the moment I awakened to what I was doing. Or maybe that was when I realized I had to lean in to learn how to lean away—or there were no realizations, only seconds in a life without purpose.

I had cramps, but my period didn't come. My boobs swelled and hurt. I pressed them at night in the dark. The ache felt good and bad all at once. I put a finger inside myself every time I went to the bathroom, hoping to see the faintest trace of blood, but, like on the toilet paper and my panties, there was nothing. After two weeks, I was freaking out. "It couldn't be, right?" I said to Sam over the phone. "I mean, we only really had sex for like a second and that was with a condom on."

"I don't know, girl. Did you ever have sex without a condom?"

"No, of course not."

"Are you sure?" I was annoyed with Sam for making me come face to face with myself at the time. I often became frustrated with condoms, was too eager for sex, too eager for skin on skin, and just risked it. I'd say things like *just for a second* and *just don't come in me* and *I'm not on birth control, this is crazy.*

"For a minute, in the tub."

"Kylie!"

"What?"

"Well, you might be pregnant. And might have an STD too."

"Whatever. I can't be, right? I mean, he was barely hard." This was before I got my IUD and my period was always irregular anyway. I walked around the city with Sam, prepped for tutoring in cafés with Sam, ran errands with Sam, all while thinking, *Maybe Tight 'n' Bright's baby is in me.* Imagine if he had been a virgin and knocked me up on his very first time. Stupider things have happened, but not by much.

I think a very specific difference may be the thing that makes people want to kill themselves. Or maybe it was just the very specific thing that made me want to kill myself. It's the difference between who you are and who you act like and who you want to be. When who you are is the same as who you want to be, who you feel you should be, you feel happy. When who you are is different from who you want to be, you are discontent, frustrated, maybe even depressed. But when who you are is different from how you act, this is when you want to kill yourself. Especially when how you act is as far away as possible from who you want to be.

I met people through yoga and climbing and a running group

I joined. I learned how to breathe with other people. I explored my many interests. I worked hard and set up my apartment in a way I liked. One time when Sam came over for coffee, shortly after she met her new boyfriend, Brad, she told me I was different now. "With all your Basic White Bitch healing. Is that all you think about all day?" She named several things that could better serve my attention. The world was in political turmoil. Racist extremism was getting more open each day. She'd seen injustices that were part of children's day-to-day lives. She'd also heard Travis had gone into the hospital, maybe for an overdose, but she never talked to him anymore and talked about her feelings about him and the drugs and the time they'd been married even less. I figured Sam was being typical Sam, that all of this would eventually come to a blowout, that she'd accuse me of being boring or abandoning her. But I was always the one worried about abandonment, not her. And really she was right, the old me who was poor all the time and resistant to spending money at all would have been shocked by the me now constantly spending money on myself, feeding the capitalist machine.

It's not that Sam and I aren't friends anymore—just that she's someone who'd very vividly been in my life, only to slowly fade away, like so many others.

Sam and I walked to a Shoppers one day. As we stood in the Family Planning section, I resisted the urge to buy condoms. It'd seem dumb with a pregnancy test and I already had an unopened box at home, but I thought it'd be so funny. I thought about the face the cashier would make and started laughing. I told Sam about the scene that was in my head, and she rolled her eyes and shoved me slightly into the shelves of boxes and boxes of condoms, red, blue, purple, and yellow. A tube of lube toppled over and I laughed harder. Fucking Tight 'n' Bright. Tight 'n' Bright, of all people.

"Here," Sam said. "The tests are over here." She stood looking at the pregnancy tests, trying to decide which one would be best for me: Clear Blue, First Response, AccuClear, Result, or the regular old store brand, which was on sale. I'd gotten paid for tutoring that morning, had a whole sixty bucks in my wallet. I was ready to go wild.

I picked up the First Response pack of two. "This is a really good value," I said to Sam. "Two tests for the price of one!" I started laughing again. Sam smiled, but looked sad. Two of her other friends had had abortions within the past three years and I'd forgotten, the way I did with everything. I only remembered later, when I was alone in bed and thinking about how she hadn't seemed herself. Wondered if I'd done something insensitive again.

Sam came with me to my place, and I peed on the test and we waited. She grabbed the test from me and poured us both vodka and juice. "So," she said. "What do you think it's going to be?"

"Just let me see it."

"No," she said, and drank. She poured herself another drink and drank again, holding the test in her hand, waving it in the air. "I want you to think about what you've done."

A PRAYER TO
THE IUD

Praise be to the IUD, which sits snuggly in Kylie's uterus. She thinks, *Oh, praise this IUD*, when her boyfriend, after a week-long breakup, follows her instructions from the couch, where she lies with freshly inserted IUD cramps. "Okay, get the big pot and fill it with water. Put it on the stove." She has to tell him where the pot is kept, even though they've been living together off and on for several months. She tells him how to make pasta and then he dumps cold canned sauce overtop of it.

"There you go!" he says, proud of himself. "Supper! Now I have to go out and meet Chris."

And then he's down the stairs and out the door, in search of Chris, who will get him high. She moans on the couch. *Praise be to the IUD.*

Praise be to the IUD, she hardly gets her period anymore. That boyfriend is gone, and her new guy, the first night, she tells him she's clean, and so is he, so because of the IUD, they can have sex without a condom. She explains that she put it in after she got back together with her old boyfriend so he couldn't knock her up.

"And now I'm the one who benefits," he jokes. He is a much sweeter man. The cramps still come, especially after sex. He rubs her back. "Was it something I did?" he asks.

"No," she says. "Just the IUD."

Oh, and there was a darker time, a time of pills swallowed that made her swell. A time when she lived only to work and to go to school and to come home to a partner, and take one pill daily, plus condoms, there couldn't be a child. The pills, they did something else too, they flattened her into numb desperation. They found her alienation and made it grow. The man she was with, he wasn't for her, and really no one was. Her periods were harsh and long. She'd bleed into the toilet, and the blood meant no child, which was what the pills were for in the first place, but the blood made her numbness fall out from her into a dark blood-clot tunnel, which only had suicide at the end. Praise be to the IUD.

Praise be to the IUD, she still thinks, as the doctor positions the needle on her arm and shoots her full of the Gardasil 9 vaccine. She can't get pregnant, but her current partner (the sweet one is gone too) doesn't really buy into monogamy. No babies, no HPV. Her list of nos is growing. The shot feels like a punch to the arm.

"Are you okay?" asks the doctor. "Do you want to lie down?" The doctor adjusts the paper on the table, moves the pillow under her head, and she surrenders.

Her friend texts her, *It's a good thing you're getting it. I'm researching and you can get HPV from grinding, from touching, from hand jobs and blow jobs, you can get HPV in your throat and it can cause cancer. You could get cervical cancer. You could die.*

Maybe I should have used condoms, she types back as her arm hurts and she gets a strange phantom cramp that either means

a) Her period is coming
b) She's ovulating
c) She sat in the wrong position
d) She slept too long in the wrong position
e) She had sex in the wrong position

f) She's carrying something heavy, or

g) It's a mystery.

Her friend texts back, *1. Condoms suck. 2. You don't understand. You can get HPV from ANYTHING.*

These shots are costing me $200 a pop.

ANYTHING.

Praise be.

Following the time of the pills, there was a time of long rage. The time of long rage was confined to a basement apartment where she lived alone. She'd check her Facebook page and be invited to a party where she knew no one. She would go and meet people. She would get too drunk. She would take people home. She no longer took the pill because what was the point without a boyfriend, what was the point when they just made you want to kill yourself. But then you stopped and you just wanted to kill yourself anyway. She sometimes used condoms, but mostly she didn't. Her anger always seemed to come out as a joke, or as drunkenness, or as a come-on, and then she'd end up in bed with someone. Sometimes she wondered why anyone ever would get close to her. There were pregnancy scares and pregnancy tests. A man she loved, but who would never look at her straight on, as if she'd hurt him. He despised her, and she wanted to give him all of herself. But then another pregnancy scare made her change her mind. This still was not the time for the IUD. She was still too angry. Sometimes people enjoy learning things the hard way.

Oh, praise this IUD. She thinks there must be nothing she wouldn't do for love. This thought makes her feel foolish, and isn't she foolish! All her friends have IUDs too, or take pills, or buy condoms, which they stash under their beds. She's bought some too, to prevent diseases, and keeps them in a box with her sex toys. One of her friends has genital warts now. Another has a yeast infection that she and her boyfriend pass back and forth. Over the summer, despite her shots, she still popped up irregular and has had to go to the gyno for Paps now every six months. She once thought that being alone would be terrible, the worst thing that could happen, and she thought she needed another person's skin on her skin, that every night she went out, it might be the start of true love. Now the person who thought that seems like an idiot, and she's afraid of cancer and approaching thirty with nothing but an IUD to show for it.

But still, she thinks most mornings. When she and her boyfriend have sex, she's relieved she doesn't have to worry, although she still gets disappointed monthly, feelings that don't connect to the brain. She thinks this thing that caused her to cramp and moan when it was first put in, that made her toss and turn, pressing her face to the waxy paper of the examination table, this thing makes her free. Let her praise it. Let her be grateful for her vast and eternal privilege.

CAVERN

***

Laura sees the cavern first, where it hovers at the ceiling of their bedroom. Through the pitch-black, almost like a tear in a night sky, she can see stars within it, and stalactites and stalagmites, which sparkle as if they are made of ancient minerals. A cave made of night.

***

It's easy to pretend that the cavern was just a projection of imagination. When she wakes up, Russ is sleeping, his lips stuck to a piece of pillowcase that he sucks when he sleeps. As if he's still a newborn instead of a thirty-five-year-old man. Her Russ. Her cat, Penelope, a ginger tabby, curled between them, really curled beside Russ, into Russ, because once they moved in together, Penelope chose Russ as her favourite. The walls of their bedroom are cream. Nothing unusual happens in a cream-coloured room. But Laura knows the cavern was real.

***

During spin class, she thinks about the cavern. She'd stayed awake most of the night, waiting for it to disappear. It wasn't large. Only took up an area of about two feet by two feet, floating above their king-size bed. Three young men in front of her chat as they cycle, loudly, trying to drown out the fitness instructor. Sometimes one reaches over to the man beside him and pushes at his shoulder, as if trying to push him off balance. The third man tries to ignore the other two and seems embarrassed by them. Laura feels nothing except a burning in her calves.

***

Russ and Laura work hard. That's one thing that drew them to each other. She liked that he'd included it in his OkCupid profile: *hard worker*. She'd said she wanted someone with their shit together, for the future. She'd also listed that she was a hard worker and one of her ex-boyfriends had made fun of her for it when they met to catch up over drinks. "That's going to attract a real nerd," he told her with a laugh. Her hand held her phone in front of his face. He told her she was shaking, moving the screen around so that he couldn't read it, and so he held her wrist, to steady her. The light from the screen casting long shadows upward, as if his eyebrows extended all the way up his forehead. That was ten years ago now. And her nerd was Russ.

***

Of course, there were things that Russ hadn't put on OkCupid. Like if he drank too much and smoked exactly three cigarettes, he'd throw up on the bathroom tiles when he'd get home. Not that it was often—just a few times in their ten years together, but each time Laura was the one to clean it up. Or like he expected Laura to be on his ass all the time. Not that she resented it. He did more than enough to make up for it. He'd brought her home a new kitten, Charles, after they'd been living together for one year, and it was a nice gesture. He knew how hurt she was by Penelope's indifference.

The cavern wakes her up next at 4:00 a.m. It's bigger. The stalagmites and stalactites are almost touching. There's sound now. She can hear it. A drip from the roof of the cavern to its floor. A faint humming as if wind is trapped somewhere deep inside it. She feels there is movement inside the cavern, but the cavern is still too dark and too small for her to see inside clearly. The twinkling isn't enough for her. She wants to see the whole thing illuminated.

***

One new thing with Laura and Russ this year is that they've stopped having sex.

***

After work one day, Laura meets up with her usual group of girlfriends. They drink, they have dinner, and then they go to a movie. The movie is long, she thinks all movies are too long now, but it's very good. It's divided into three parts, and each part tells its own story. The viewer has to figure out how the parts fit together. "It was a little highbrow for me," her friend Sarah admits as they leave the theatre. "But one thing I love about arty movies is all the full-frontal." Her friends all laugh and she tries to laugh along too. She feels a twinge as she remembers the dick shot. *So I do still have a clit*, she thinks.

***

She's the one who started this whole no-sex thing. She knows it. One night after they'd both had really hard weeks, they came home from a party. He asked her if she wanted to make love, and she said yes. When they first were together, somehow it always just happened, like in the movies, clothes falling off and her legs lifting up and his body pressing on top of her, that mouth that sucks pillowcases on her mouth. That night, she said yes because she wanted to say yes. She said yes because she thought he wanted her to say yes. She said yes because she wanted him to want her to say yes. But it was painful. As soon as he went to put his dick into her, she closed up like a fist.

"You're dry, honey," he said. "Do you need me to turn you on?"

He'd tried going down on her for a minute or two.

The fist in her pussy tightened further.

"Just try it," she said. So he did.

Afterwards she cried. Sometimes she did that, although she never really had with Russ.

"What's wrong?" he said.

He always kept making it worse.

***

One way to think more about sex is wanting to stop thinking about sex.

***

Their town, Pettering, is between two large cities. Laura works in one, and Russ works in the other, but other than work, Pettering has everything they need. Two movie theatres, one outlet of each grocery store chain, several bars and restaurants, and a book club Laura joined and then quit. A community centre with a skating rink and a gym, and enough trees and forest to make everyone feel that their lives are different from those in the city, despite the subdivisions that kept creeping in. Laura knows she has nothing to complain about. Pettering is safe. When she and Russ have children, they will be able to walk home without worrying, even late at night. She wishes she had grown up somewhere with so much to do. She has wonderful friends. She never has no one to talk to. She and Russ have been happy in Pettering, happy for five years. And if they ever aren't happy, they can always go into either city, spend the night out, and return exhausted.

***

In the morning, Russ locks himself in the bathroom, while Laura rummages around downstairs doing dishes, making breakfast, sipping cup after cup of coffee. Like she always does before a big day at work, setting the cup down hard on the counter, slamming the pots into their drawer. He knows when to stay out of Laura's way. First, he takes his dump. Then he looks at porn on his iPad. Then he showers and comes down the stairs. This is his private ritual.

***

Work goes late. Laura has to stay and finish a presentation brief before heading to the gym and squeaks into the late spin class. She grabs a wrap on the way home, eating it as she drives. The endorphins from her workout and the beans and avocado from her wrap fill her with an energy she hasn't felt all month. She starts to think about the man from the movie, the full-frontal scene. She thinks about the men in spin class. She thinks about a woman with a tight purple sweater who smiled at her in Zehrs on the weekend. She starts to get wet.

When she reaches home, Russ is asleep. He's rolled on his side in the fetal position, the blanket pulled up to his ears. She remembers that today he was supposed to go to the doctor to get his knee scoped, but she forgot to text him to see how it went.

There is a lump on her side of the bed. She lifts the blanket and finds Penelope curled there. She climbs into bed, Penelope between her and Russ. She is asleep within minutes.

***

Honestly, Russ thinks it's stupid to feel hurt by a cat.

***

One night after she's fallen asleep, he wakes up from a vivid dream. He can see the cavern, floating in their bedroom. The cave, the sparkling cones that descend from its ceiling and jut from its floor. A hole like a night sky, suspended over the bed. But Russ has never been a figurative thinker, and he doesn't know what this appearance means, except that he instantly knows it's come from her, Laura. She always has strange ideas, a different mind than his. It was something he'd adored, in the beginning.

***

The cavern exists not just between her and Russ, it exists in her and has always existed in her.

***

The next night, Russ hugs Laura as soon as she comes in from work. "Missed you lately," he says, and runs his hand over her butt. He takes her briefcase from her hand and drops it to the ground. He takes the groceries from her other hand and does the same thing. He tries to kiss her, forcefully, with tongue.

"Russ," Laura says. "There's ice cream bars in there."

He loves ice cream bars. He helps her unpack the groceries and load up the fridge and eats an ice cream bar. It's covered in chocolate and almonds, his favourite. She always remembers.

They have dinner and stream a movie through their Apple TV. Once they are both in bed, Laura begins to kiss him again, as if it's still the moment she walked through the door. She inches her pelvis toward his as they kiss, closer each time. Something about flexing these muscles, acknowledging that a part of her is drawn to him like this, like something red and burning and needing so much to be pressed, turns her on even more. She reaches her hand down the front of his pyjama pants and expects to find him hard, but his penis is still soft.

"One second," he says. He reaches his own hand down into his PJ bottoms and starts to jerk at his dick. He rolls over and stares at the ceiling, trying to concentrate on the feeling. "I don't think it's going to happen," he says.

"Look," Laura says. Over the bed, the cavern is floating. It now takes up the whole ceiling. Laura looks at Russ, who looks back at Laura. They are both seeing it. Both know that it's in the room with them. They hold hands as the mineral deposits twinkle.

***

Now that the cavern is bigger, the sound of the dripping and whistling is louder. Shapes move inside the stalagmites and stalactites. "Do you see them?" Laura asks. Bodies pace inside the spikes that descend from the ceiling. A woman and man, both with greying hair, cling to each other. In one, a man stabs a young girl repeatedly. In another, a middle-aged man remains alone, his arms wrapped around himself. Two women sit on the ground back-to-back, as if they are waiting for something. In fact, even the violent man and bleeding girl look like they are waiting, although the cavern is just something they exist in, exists around them.

"What do you mean?" says Russ.

***

Laura has met up with her ex-boyfriend twice since she and Russ got together and both times they had sex. "Fucked," her ex-boyfriend clarified. It never was her intention, but she "knew it was a possibility," he told her every time she curled into his back, her forehead resting on his spine, her arms circling around him. She cried, feeling guilty and worthless, wondering how dinner, how drinks, brought them both here, but had never brought them into a bedroom with cream-coloured walls that they co-owned.

***

Russ and Laura's next fight is long and ends with threats of going their separate ways. Laura says it's about getting another cat. Russ says it's about how Laura thinks only about herself and never thinks about what her words say. Both of them want to mention the cavern, how Laura barely sleeps, and want to blame it on the other. Laura thinks that if she were alone, there never would have been a cavern. For each couple that she saw waiting in the cavern, she saw another life for herself, some worse, some better, but all made her wonder, why these walls, this house, this job, this Russ.

That night, Russ takes his food into the living room to eat and watches television until he falls asleep on the couch. His lips search out a corner of the pillow. Laura would find it disgusting if she didn't find it so cute. She loves when Russ is just peaceful-baby-sleeping Russ. She knows she doesn't look the same while she sleeps. She can't—she always has too many nightmares.

***

Russ opens his eyes to the cavern. He's in the living room, on the couch. Penelope is lying on the floor beside his hand, which has drifted from where it'd rested on his lap. The cavern seems deeper than before, blacker. The stalagmites and stalactites join, their minerals hardened and fused together. Inside, he sees people like Laura had seen, sees even more. Even the people have more people in them. Each person is different from Laura's. Toward the back, a group of three people argue, two men and a woman. Two men, one with scars all along his back. But there's no violence in Russ's cavern, and in fact, the people are happy to be there, he thinks. As he thinks that, the cavern grows even more. Laura sleeps peacefully, alone in the other room. He wonders how much bigger it will grow, how something so beautiful came from him.

The doors don't sit flush on their hinges.
You are swollen, hard, open, erect.

A STORY ABOUT OUR FRIENDS LANA AND TIA

Lana has been working ten hours already. The clock says 8:00 p.m., and she knows Tia is going on her first date. Clarification: her first date with someone who is not Lana. Clarification: her first date with someone who is not Lana since she met Lana.

Lana agreed to this. Lana needs us to remind her: *Lana, remember you agreed to this.*

There is a long line at Hallmark. It's getting close to Christmas, and this is what days are like if you're a manager. If you're a manager who cares about her job. If you're a manager who cares about her job despite Tia thinking it's dumb and corporate.

"How is working retail dumb and corporate?"

"It's dumb and corporate the way you're doing it."

Rude.

Lana does wish sometimes that she was more like Tia. Although she'd never admit that to Tia. She likes telling Tia what she admires about her, without admitting that sometimes they are also the things she envies about her. Her inventiveness, that she always has good ideas, and could be good at, really, whatever she wanted to do. Tia says she thinks they have different love languages, and none of these compliments ever seems to stick. It's one of their problems.

But Tia has always been very clear—opening up the relationship isn't about being in a relationship that has problems. "All relationships have problems, and my new relationships will too. It's healthy to want to explore other options. I mean, not options. I mean, love is something that's meant to be shared and I think we need to be sharing with more people than just each other." She framed it as an experiment, an idea. She said it wasn't an ultimatum.

But then of course she brought up the fact that Lana is in love with her strap-on.

Let's be real, Lana doesn't really know if she's in love with her strap-on. But that's what Tia tells her. She says she feels as if Lana could just be alone with the strap-on and she'd be happy. She says that Lana has no interests but the strap-on. That the strap-on is her real long-term partner.

Tia complains that the strap-on is what controls the way they have sex. That Lana doesn't understand that not all sex is penetrative, which just blows Tia's mind because she doesn't know how Lana has gotten through three committed relationships before Tia without this coming up.

(Although it has taken Tia two and a half years, one of which was in couples therapy, to finally say this.)

Tia has needs. Needs that are not fulfilled by having a third, soft, latexy, pink partner in the room with them. Needs that are not fulfilled by watching Lana walk around in the special way she does once she's wearing the strap-on, so that it bounces up and down with every step, until they both are laughing. Lana loves when their laughter turns into sex. She loves making Tia laugh. But even though we all think of Tia as the funny one of the two of them, as having a dry sense of humour (which Lana sometimes thinks is a nice way of saying a mean sense of humour), she prefers some serious passion over Lana's silliness.

They aren't the first of our friends to go to couples therapy, but they are the first to talk openly about it. Or, at least, Tia is the first to talk openly about it. The therapist had asked them if maybe it was better if they parted ways.

"Of course not. I love Lana."

Lana had been ready to cry. "I didn't know. If she did. I mean, I knew, but…" She'd felt all her emotions pull to the tip of her when the therapist had suggested that. "I love Tia. She's so fierce and strong."

Tia had rolled her eyes.

"What do you love about Lana?"

"Lana?"

"Yes, Tia."

"Lana takes care of me."

This isn't Lana's first non-monogamous relationship, but what Tia wants is different from Lana's previous relationships—Tia wants to be free to be Tia, to not be in any social situation and feel as if she needs to control herself, limit herself, not explore new connections and feelings because of her devotion to Lana. "Sometimes it feels like I'm in a small dark room, and no one is in there, not even you, and there is no handle, no door, no windows, and the room keeps getting smaller."

For Lana, the relationship has always felt different, although she understands the room feeling, the walls coming in closer and closer. But Lana always felt that if she stared hard enough at the walls, they would give way to another, bigger room, that that was what love really was, feeling as if you've reached the boundary and then going further, realizing there was more to you than you ever could know.

"You've always been the romantic," Tia said, and kissed Lana playfully. Closed mouth. But the softness different than when Tia is mad, her lips like two hard pieces of rubber bumping against Lana's mouth. When Tia kisses Lana like she wants to, her lips feel as if they dissolve into hers. Lana would do anything for that feeling.

Lana's first relationship had been a triangle with a man and woman. Or really, a boy and a girl, since they were all in high school. The boy and girl had been dating first, and then Lana became friends with both of them when she changed schools. She was impressed by their devotion to each other. She liked the way they took care of each other. The girl was perfect in every way, a bright smile, she paid attention when Lana talked to her, sometimes held her hand when Lana told her something very serious. The three of them, they felt like adults with the way they talked, about life and death and their families. Both the boy and the girl told Lana about their parents' divorces, about fights that lasted days, and Lana told them about food. How she felt that food was something that wrapped itself around her brain and squeezed. That she always either had too much or too little, and that sometimes she needed to eat just to not feel alone with her father. She didn't know why food was like that for her, something to hold her. But her friends understood and they loved her for her honesty.

The triangle relationship echoed in the unrequited feelings she often experienced as an adult, the feeling of being perfectly a part of something, yet not quite. And while Lana did have three well-functioning relationships before hers with Tia, something about that sexless triangle relationship had more of a lasting positive impact than her other relationships. Honestly, Lana has never felt liked. She didn't feel liked by her father, she didn't feel liked by her first girlfriend or her second or her third. She's always felt as though she has to work so hard to be liked. Even with Tia. Especially with Tia. But it wasn't like that with the boy and the girl.

None of them had sex, although the girl and Lana had kissed. The guy and the girl still went on their own dates, but the boy would call Lana some nights and they'd talk until they were almost falling asleep. They made each other presents and said "I love you" whenever they parted or hung up the phone. During the summer, when school was out and Lana couldn't convince her father to drive her to visit them, the couple broke up and the relationship faded away. As Lana lay in her bed, heartbroken and listening to her Discman, sometimes she told herself that it had really just been a friendship. That the "I love yous," the conversations, falling asleep on the phone, kisses, hadn't meant anything. They were all just kids playing a game. Real relationships were between two people anyway. She'd only been a hanger-on, a third wheel. That's all.

Lana didn't think about that relationship for a long time. Until she met Tia. Right on their first date, Tia mentioned that she'd be into a non-traditional arrangement, and the triangle relationship came back, the sweetness of it. "Of course, something like that has to be good for everyone, so it's not a deal breaker," Tia said. And for the first year and a half, it wasn't.

A long line snakes out the door. A woman joins the line holding ten rolls of wrapping paper—it's *buy ten get ten per cent off*—and within a second, one goes shooting out the middle. With the middle gone, the rolls fall into each other and the woman can't catch them. They scatter across the floor. The person in front of the woman looks behind him and shrugs. He's holding a teddy bear, several cards, and a gift bag. The woman behind her huffs in annoyance, five rolls underneath each arm herself. People skip over the fallen rolls as they beeline toward a wall displaying holiday ornaments. Lana is talking with someone at the cash but manages to signal to one of the teenage short-term hires to go gather the rolls.

And while all this happens, Lana is imagining Tia.

Tia smiling into the eyes of another woman. Tilting her chin up, while she thinks and listens to a woman who is not

Lana. And then going home to the other woman's apartment. Lana sees her mouth on the woman's mouth. Her mouth on the woman's nipples, her tongue sliding along her stomach, her fingers. Lana imagines the fingers on the woman's thigh for a long time. She tries to imagine the woman as someone she might also be drawn to, one of our friends even, or an ex, but the images don't arouse her. They make a pit of growling in her stomach.

"Let's get pizza," Lana says to her assistant manager, on the till beside her. "On me."

"The kids will love that," the assistant manager says back, and they both scan through the next customers.

We try to all get together once a month, but people have jobs, people have passions and careers, and sometimes friendship falls to the wayside. Mike and Kyle even adopted a baby last year, and Jen and Dan's kid is turning four. Our friends sink into their couches and can't remember the last time they made it to the bar.

Even when you get everyone out, people are mercurial. One second everyone is gelling, and the next, it seems as if we barely know each other, or people are all checking their phones, or the always-on-time people have to wait over a half-hour for the always-late people, or Lana and Tia slide into the booth, shaking snow from their hats and scarves as they come in, which melts all over our paper menus, spotting them. These are the small annoyances of friendship.

Friends always know when something is wrong, even if we don't always talk about it. For instance. We notice that when Lana takes off her scarf, her elbow pokes Tia. She gives Lana *a look*, and then it becomes one of those days we'll all seem as if we barely know each other because we actually know each other too well.

Tia is at a restaurant called Defina. She'd been into her date for a while—she was a friend's ex-girlfriend who sometimes hung around when we'd all go out. She had come to Mike and Kyle's two weeks ago, to celebrate their first year as parents. She'd brought a present and tried to talk a little bit to everyone, despite not knowing anyone very well. It showed good manners. Good character. Tia liked that. She also is beautiful in that perfect-cute way—dark straight hair she never has to do anything to, eyes that squint when she laughs. Tia doesn't tell her how long she's liked her, why she likes her. Why give someone a compliment when you're already complimenting her with your time and attention? Instead, she asks her date how her day was. Her date picks up an olive and bites into it with her two front teeth. She twists the olive, her teeth resting against its hard pit, and then pulls. The olive in her hand is missing half its flesh and the half-naked pit points toward her, accusingly. "I used to hate olives," she says. "When I was little. I hated my dad for asking my mom to get them at the grocery store. Nothing smelled worse than that olive cart."

"You ever eaten olives in Greece?" Tia says.

"No, I'm too poor to go anywhere. When were you there?"

"There's nothing like it. Olives in Greece, olives in Italy. We travelled a lot. My dad worked all over. Never had roots anywhere. But I got to see the whole world. I didn't appreciate it then. I just wanted to be in North America with big grocery stores and olive carts."

"Well, you're here now!"

"Yeah, I am. And now I'm also too poor to go anywhere."

Tia thinks of Lana at home and smiles. She's somehow forgotten that Lana would not be at home waiting for her, that she's wrapping up hour eleven and getting ready for hour twelve at the card store. Tia will tell Lana about the olive, about how at that moment she's repulsed by imagining how her date's fingers will smell after touching the olive, after being half in her mouth. She thinks about how the gesture of her date is charming, but her date knows it's charming, which makes it uncharming again. She wants to hear Lana tell her she's too judgmental as she pats the spot beside her on the couch. Tia would climb up onto the couch beside Lana, and Lana would cover Tia's feet with a little bit of the blanket she would be reading under. She knows that parts of Tia are always cold, especially in winter.

Her date is telling her about all the places she wants to travel to one day. Tia reaches out her leg, so her foot rests gently on the woman's shin.

Lana bought the strap-on alone. She had just broken up with her first serious girlfriend and felt adrift. Something about that first relationship had allowed Lana to look at herself in the mirror and not criticize herself so heavily. Now the voice was back, telling her she was fat and had an awful personality, and, like her father always said, she was difficult. What did it mean to be difficult? It must have been why her relationship had ended. Or her ex found someone more beautiful. Despite not having evidence yet, she was left with a vague feeling of being replaced.

Lana was selling clothes then, not cards and gifts, at a store down on Queen Street. She walked along after her shift was over with too much daylight left and nowhere to go. Whenever she got into a relationship, she always disappeared into a relationship hole, dropped her friends one by one. We'd all hated that girlfriend and wouldn't talk to her if Lana brought her out, so they tended to stay at her apartment. The time in her day was now oppressive. The street in front of her, crowded with couples and people who wanted to spend time with each other, was oppressive. She was also filled with an aimlessness that made her realize that she could be anyone, do anything, that she had no more restrictions on her now that she was alone.

So she ducked into a sex shop.

Lana had never had a vibrator or a dildo before, although

she had thought about it sometimes. Mostly when she had dry skin in winter and didn't feel like putting her fingers inside herself. During her relationship, she'd stopped masturbating more or less, but now that it was over, Lana felt herself digging into a long period of being alone. Maybe forever, the voice even said, if she got what she deserved.

Several rubber dicks penetrated the air. Long metal tubes and glass rods were locked underneath a case. She ran her hands along a wall covered with leather and whips and harnesses. "I don't want anything colourful," Lana said to the woman at the front counter, looking around nervously. "Like, I don't want to feel like it could belong to an alien." The woman glowered at her and pointed out some dildos that were different skin tones. She explained the difference between the ones that vibrated and the ones that didn't. Lana began to giggle, seeing them all there. The ones with balls, she found especially funny. A giant pink silicone member pointed at her. The saleswoman frowned again. A sign on the wall said, "We don't make fun of your junk, so don't make fun of ours." Lana couldn't stop laughing. She imagined a sales associate making the sign on a computer, printing it out, trimming the sides so the paper just framed the words, and then taping it to the wall. Noticing it was tilted too much to one side, then peeling it off and taping it so it was straight. The seriousness of it all made it even more funny to Lana.

How immature.

She tried on a harness in the store's change room. She put the pink dildo into the harness and arched her back, jutting the dildo in front of her. She gave it a flick like she used to with those springy doorstops at her dad's house, making them spronggggg until her dad told her to knock it off. She started to laugh again.

Altogether, it cost more than three hundred dollars—money that was supposed to go to rent or groceries. Lana knew it meant she'd be eating rice and drinking black coffee for the rest of the month. She didn't care. Her bag was loaded up with lube and the harness and the pink dildo. She'd always thought that if she got a dildo it'd be the same skin colour as her, so she could pretend it'd grown from her. But the pink dildo had been the only one into the joke.

Half a decade later, when Tia met Lana through our group of friends, she told Lana stories about working briefly at a sex shop over on Yonge Street. When you first meet anyone, you grab for these details of shared interest, and Lana asked question after question about working there, and Tia found a funny way to talk about all the kink Lana would ever want to hear about.

But Tia found sex toys absolutely boring and worked hard to forget the few months she'd spent working at the store. Now she works at an office. And likes it. She likes getting dressed up for work and checking her hair in the mirror. But while she's been working as an office assistant since before she met Lana, she knows she might not stay an office assistant. She's been a postal worker, a merchandizer, a dog walker, a tutor, a jewellery maker. She's also an avid knitter with a following on her Instagram account. Like Lana says, Tia can do anything, anything that doesn't require her to go back to school for more than two years, but even then, sometimes Tia dreams. A master's and a PhD. Professor Tia. Dr. Tia. There are so many versions of herself she hasn't even gotten to explore yet.

At the card store, the customers are getting ferocious. It nears 9:45 p.m., the last fifteen minutes for customers to shop. One of the teen hires comes into the backroom sobbing. Shopping bags for the front cash are stacked on the shelf right at the top, and Lana, not tall enough, is using a wrapping-paper roll to try to push them down. "What's wrong?"

"This man told me we're a bunch of fuck-ups. 'Cause we aren't open longer."

"Oh, what an asshole. It's not about you, honey."

"Can't we do anything? Tell him we won't serve him?"

To be young and outraged when people treat you like shit. "I think it'd just make things worse, but if you want, I can deal with him."

Lana goes onto the shop floor and braces herself. The man is nowhere to be seen. In fact, other than the customers in line, no one is shopping. An eerie lull. Lana knows it won't last. She puts the stack of shopping bags behind the counter and leans against it. Her feet are throbbing. She imagines Tia, a foot in her mouth, but the foot is small, dainty. Her date's. Tia licks and licks and begs. The cash beeps, beeps, beeps as Lana's assistant manager rings customers through.

And then, a crash.

Lana gets to the woman first. The cardboard back-wall display of non-name-brand ornaments has fallen, and the woman is trying to hold the cardboard up. The aisle is deserted. If shoppers had been there with the woman, they are gone now, moved on to Carlton Cards or Dynamite or Toys"R"Us. The woman is frail, elderly, and her arms quiver under the weight of the cardboard and ornaments.

"Are you all right?" Lana takes the weight from the woman, pushes it up. One of the teen hires comes over and together she and Lana pull the wall out of the way.

The woman's sweater caught on one of the wall hooks and rode up. She tugs it down to collect herself, smooths the fabric down. She reaches out for her cane, which the teen hire hands to her. Lana smiles at the woman. "Are you okay? Can I get you anything?"

"Nothing broken," the woman says. She examines a scrape on the back of her hand, but it's not bleeding. "Goodness, though, that was a scare."

Lana hands the woman the ornament she had been trying to get down. "We would have gotten it down for you if you'd just asked," Lana says, keeping her voice controlled, trying not to think about what could have happened if something harder had fallen on the customer's head when the display came down.

"Oh, I didn't want to bother you. You're so busy this time of year."

"Still, we should have helped you, so I'd like to give you twenty-five per cent off today. Can I give you twenty-five per cent off?"

"Oh my, well, thank you," the woman says, and adds a few more things to her purchase. "Twenty-five per cent is so wonderful, I really appreciate it, especially since I got this scratch here, and such a fright."

"You're right, thirty per cent," Lana says, "at least on these items right here." And rings them up.

"I hope you have a nice young man to keep you warm in this cold," the woman says before leaving, even though Lana definitely, definitely looks forty-five.

There are no good people left in this world, Lana thinks.

"That was nice of you," the teen hire says.

"Meh, I just didn't want her to sue," Lana says. "Now I'm going to have to call head office."

Lana walks to the back and calls her district manager. "What a fucking day," she says, and takes a bite of cold pizza while her boss talks her down, tells her how great today's sales have been.

Tia takes the woman to her favourite bar. "Have you ever wondered if you could be with one person, only one person for the rest of your life?"

Her date smiles, leans in, kisses her. "I know I could," her date says.

"I feel like I want to love so much, I want to love as many people as I can handle."

"I want to love someone who is especially mine."

"Well, you're not going to get that with me," Tia says. "You know what my situation is."

"But maybe we could change that," says the woman, leaning in again, putting her head on Tia's shoulder. They curl up together in one side of a booth. Tia holds her hand and rubs the skin with her thumb. "You have what I like to call a wandering soul. You must have some Sagittarius in your chart."

Tia knows this would make Lana laugh. "Nope, nothing but Virgo and Libra."

"Well, you're a wanderer."

"Maybe." Tia drinks her whisky quickly. "Why be here then? If I'm a wanderer and you're not okay with what I'm willing to give?"

"I'm curious," the woman says, and they start kissing again.

Tia will not sleep with her tonight. She knows that already. She may never even see her again. She doesn't like her date's olive-covered fingers rubbing all over her skin, but she does like the way she tastes, like her fruity drink and garlic. But all love takes a certain letting go that Tia isn't ready to do yet.

And on some level, she is never ready.

"You don't want to use it anymore? Okay, we won't use it. I just thought it was fun."

"It's more than that, and you know it."

"No, I don't know it. How can I be in love with that? It's a thing!"

"People can be in love with anything. Remember that

documentary? And you said so yourself."

"I said I love it, not that I'm in love with it."

"What's the difference anyway?"

"Tia, I love you. You."

"People can be in love with more than one person *or thing* at a time."

"Fine, if that's what you want, fine."

"It has to be what we both want."

"It's what I want, fine, it's what I want."

Tia will go home and tell Lana all about it. Lana will listen and put her arm around her on the couch. Lana always listens. As Tia nears the house they share, her pace quickens. Nothing has ever turned Tia on more than a good long conversation.

I MOVED OUT WHEN I CAUGHT HIM WITH THE DOG

I moved out when I caught him with the dog. Or, that's not true because really I tried to understand his fixation… We went to counselling and I tried to see the dog the way I had before, with a name and a personality, but I just couldn't. I gave the dog to my sister, who still lives on our family's farm out in the country. I told myself that I gave it away because I wanted it to be safe while we worked on things, but I couldn't stand looking into the eyes of what had become my husband's furry fleshlight.

In therapy, he tried to explain it and I tried to understand, and I told him that he could go to jail for something like that, didn't he know, didn't he care, and he smiled at me in this way he had whenever I'd caught him doing something wrong, the way he'd always smiled since he was a little kid and faced confrontation. He explained that it also went back to childhood and he tried, he really tried, to get away from it all but he had just loved the dog so much and it was difficult when the dog got all worked up, when he wanted it the way he did. I said, "You can't be serious," and looked at the therapist, who never even wrote anything down, just watched us. My husband said maybe he shouldn't have pets. The therapist thought that was a very surface-level way of dealing with the problem. I begged them both, "How do I get to the point where I understand something like this?"

The therapist asked me if I had any sexual secrets that I

could share with my husband, and I said that sometimes when I walked down the street I imagined all the men couldn't keep their cocks in their pants and soon I was surrounded by dicks, with one pressing into my back and one pressing into my hair and one in my mouth, all while I was on my way to shop at Loblaws, was that what she fucking meant? Or that the first three months we were married, when we stopped having sex and I gained fifteen pounds, I walked to the sex club every day, hoping to get the courage to go in so someone would fuck me, is that what she meant? Was that a sexy enough secret for her? All those times I'd said I was taking classes in marketing, that's what I was doing. My husband didn't say anything, of course, and looked at his hands. And I knew he never actually looked at his hands when he was embarrassed or ashamed, that it was just something he was doing because it made him look humbled, when really I could have said anything, and he would be the same person he always was.

When we got home, it was late, so I put a pizza in the oven and he took out a beer and drank it all before the pizza was done. We sat on the same couch and watched the same show and ate one half each. We then decided to go to sleep, although most nights I no longer slept, I just remembered the same memory over and over, well two really, first of Christmas, two years into the marriage and him giving me the dog, how happy I was because I had always loved animals so much, even wanted to be a vet when I was young. It was my dog. And then remembering walking in, home early from work, and seeing.

That night after therapy, he said, "I think we're making real progress, Penny," and slid his hand up my nightie and felt my ass and the small of my back. I'd turned away from him, the way I did every night. I don't know why I still slept in the same bed as him instead of making him sleep on the couch. I guess I figured if we were going to work it out, I might as well try to keep everything as normal as possible. He rubbed the small of my back and the top of my ass for several minutes and I didn't roll over even though I could already feel the heat from his hard dick. He said into my ear, "I love the little blond hairs you have here." That's when I decided to move out.

I didn't have time to find a new apartment, and I was between jobs. I'd been teaching college, courses in marketing, like the ones I'd said I'd been taking those few years ago. I'd started crying in front of the class one day and accidentally told a colleague what had happened with my husband as I swore out loud about all the failing papers I had to grade, and the colleague talked to my boss because apparently I was making people uncomfortable, and then my boss decided to look more into me and what I was doing teaching and found out that I actually hadn't technically finished any schooling, just dabbled here and there. And so I was out of a job. Transitioning into a new career, I told people. I figured there must be something I could do. So I went to my sister. I needed family at a time like this.

Of course, there was the dog, as soon as I showed up, greeting me at the door, wagging its disgusting tail. "Get it away from me!" I shouted before even saying hello to my sister. She took it to the basement.

"You know, he's a really lovely dog."

"I don't want to even look at it. The whole time I'm here."

She hugged me then. She was two years older than me, and she smelled like the sage soap she made from scratch. Always showing off and making things.

The farm was our grandmother's originally, not something Lisa built on her own. Dairy and eggs, chickens and horses. Somehow Lisa knew how to keep it all in balance, knew how many workers to hire, and the farm was more or less sustainable. Every night, we ate a meal of things from the farm with all the workers before they headed home for the day. In another life, Lisa said, she would've been a chef, but it was too late for another life now. And what was I doing except starting another life. It had to be possible, didn't it? Lisa didn't even think about it more than a second, just crammed another piece of bread down her throat.

It lay in the doorway to the dining room watching us, hoping for scraps. "Why didn't you put it away," I said to her quietly, so the farmhand beside her wouldn't hear. She didn't say anything, so I slammed my fork and knife down and went to bed.

"My sister," I heard her apologizing as I walked away. "She's going through a difficult time."

Lisa knew I couldn't do much, but put me to work with the horses. They were what I'd always loved as a girl. Learned to ride there. I'd had a favourite horse, a chestnut Oldenburg stallion that my grandparents used as a stud. When I walked up to him, I could see myself in the reflection of his eye, approaching upside down. He'd bow his head to me, and I'd pat him on the nose. He was hard to control, but I'd liked his wildness.

The hands left me alone for the most part. I'd thought that maybe one of them would scoop me up and wash the stink of my husband right off me with a prolonged sex adventure, but they avoided me as if I were something spoiled. Before going out to work for the day, I looked at myself in the mirror. What was wrong with me? A little pudge here and there, but my eyes were fierce and I looked like I was ready to bend over and be wild with someone. But after working for a day or two, I lost interest in all that anyway. The hands didn't have anything to say, and for some reason, when I was out with the horses, that was the time that I let myself miss my husband.

I had to muck stalls, and feed the horses their hay and

their grains, and keep track of feeding and cleaning schedules, but the part I enjoyed most was grooming. I always started with this one old mare that looked as if she'd already been through about ten lives, her hair like the one on my horse when I was young, but flecked with grey. I used the curry brush to work over the coat, avoiding her sensitive face and legs. I felt her tension before she relaxed and gave in to the grooming, her eyes following me wherever I moved. Then, using a dandy brush, I flicked up a cloud of dust from her hair, smoothed the hair with a body brush, and moved on to untangling the mane and tail. When I was done with her hooves, one at a time, she was beautiful. It all came back so easily. Lisa had five horses there and would often board others for extra money. I became used to the excitement of new arrivals, learning their new personalities and how to handle them.

"You're good with them," one hand told me after I'd been there for a few weeks. He was tall with large hands and long fingers, a good hard straight nose. But I just continued to focus on the work, didn't even look up. I didn't want anyone to touch me or talk to me during those moments. Late that night, as I heard the dog pace in front of the door and scratch, trying to find a way into the room, I regretted this. All I'd ever wanted when I was living with my husband was some man to talk to me and then fuck me sideways, but, oh well, I thought, maybe people really do change.

I started running in the early mornings before getting the horses' days started. I'd run down the dirt drive and then along the street lined with fields until I hit the encroaching subdivisions. Fathers were leaving the houses, heading to work, some of them hauling sleeping kids to daycares. Mothers were tucking in the edges of their crumpled blouses before jumping into vans. By the time I reached the subdivisions, I was sweating through my shirt and disgusting, with strands of my hair escaping my ponytail and sticking to me, and I'd take a little breather there.

One day, a woman was pushing a kid into a sedan's car seat as I slowed and stopped, walking and staring at all these people continuing with their lives. The woman stared back at me, which almost never happened. She yelled something at me, leaning her elbow against the top of the car. I pointed at myself and shrugged. She moved closer to me, forgetting to buckle in her kid, who kicked and thrashed in his seat, little monster.

"Are you her?" she said to me as she got closer. "Get the fuck away from here. Stay away from my family."

I started to say something, but she turned and rushed back to the sedan, slamming her kid into the seat, snapping shut the buckle. She ducked into the car and drove past me, and I swore she called me a whore through the car window, clueless idiot, but I was already running, back to the farm and my horses.

That night, after we had finished dinner and the hands had gone home to their families or out drinking or picking up girls, Lisa cleared the table and brought out another bottle of wine and asked me to sit with her in the living room. I found my old favourite chair, where I used to sit when visiting Grandma, and she sat right next to the fireplace, feeding in log after log, building up and then poking at the fire. She poured wine for both of us, and I'd already had a couple with dinner and sipped my third one down fast and sloppily.

I told Lisa the story about my morning run, the women in the subdivision. How she'd accosted me. I'd meant it to be funny, but it came out another way. "Some people have no sense of boundaries," I said. "They just put their issues onto everything they see."

"Well, getting cheated on can turn you into an animal," Lisa said. "I've been thinking a lot about it lately. About April. Since you came here."

She'd never really talked much about April before—our parents hadn't been all that welcoming. Before he died, my dad never went over to the farm to visit if April was home and gave her teasing, horrible nicknames. He'd teased my husband too, always purposely misremembering his name as Steve instead of Scott. But I knew it was no comparison, although I wasn't able to offer much support: I was married already, building my career slowly out of imagined milestones, trying to make my husband happy and pretending I was happy. When April left Lisa for another woman, I didn't even ask about it. I let her figure herself out. You have to understand, that's how Lisa was, is; she was on her own and always had been.

Lisa drank her wine down. "I think I had a drinking problem after she left," she said. "It's just, Penny, I know how you're feeling about everything. It hits you hard. But I knew it was coming. You can just tell."

"I couldn't," I said.

"But there must have been signs of the betrayal."

"To be honest, I was just trying to earn a living. God knows what he did with his days."

"Well, that's what I'm saying. That's how I felt. Growing up too. A family, it's supposed to make you feel like you belong somewhere, but you still feel lonely—at least, I did."

I just drank more wine.

"Anyway, you meet someone and they say, 'You're not alone! I promise I'm here!' And you get used to that, but then something happens and you don't notice at first but then you do and you're alone again except the other person is still there."

"Well, I don't know anything about that."

"But then she actually left...and that's a different loneliness. Part of me always wonders if we hadn't been monogamous, if then maybe she would have been honest with me, maybe I didn't respect the way she needed to be, but she's married to her now. I don't know. Monogamous or not, there's no way to pretend that if you weren't loved, not truly loved, that it would go differently. But I wanted… I thought it would work for me. I thought we'd start a family." Lisa was crying now and pouring herself another glass.

"You have so many problems," I said, and finished my wine and went upstairs.

As if there could ever be love. When I thought back to the first days of being in love with my husband, it was just a rush of complication I felt. From certain angles, he repulsed me. From others, I wanted nothing more than to lie in his arms. He stuck with me, and at times I thought that was enough. Not so much love, just making up your mind, but even that could be easily changed. And that's what Lisa had experienced. It wasn't my fault she was still delusional, thinking of it all as either love or not love, as something grand instead of the smallest of things.

It came and scratched at my door. I opened the door and stared at the creature. The dog looked up at me with those damn brown eyes, and I thought of how my husband had said he'd been asking for it, that the dog got worked up. Well, I'd asked for it too sometimes and it'd never gotten me anything. I started to walk to the bed. It trailed after me. "Stop," I said. "Stay."

It patiently sat down, just like I'd taught it.

"Lie down." It lay in the doorway, just outside my room, and I let it stay there, pushing its body gently as I closed the door.

That night I googled bestiality. I read two lines from the Wikipedia entry before closing it. I lay in my bed, thinking of the things he'd revealed to me when we were in front of a therapist. He'd felt inadequate staying at home all day—he'd never been able to hold down a job. I was the one out hustling and trying to make our life livable. He said part of it was that the dog understood him, that he felt this painful desire to be understood. He'd never told me this, not even in the beginning. I'd asked him if he'd ever spent time trying to understand me. I'd never signed up to support both of us. Was that what marriage really was, locking yourself up so tight with another person even though all of their secrets and betrayals could easily destroy you?

I got out of bed. I opened the door, and it was still laying across the entranceway, head resting on its paws. "Get," I said to it. "Get out of here!" I nudged it with my foot, but it stayed. I wanted to give it a kick, but I couldn't. Part of me still remembered when I used to call myself its mother.

I think that was when I started to dream of the horses. Six horses stood side by side, my eyes so close to their coats. Chestnut brown. I was looking for the dirt. I spent the entire night pulling dust from their coats with my raw fingertips.

Another dream I had, I was having sex with a man in a grey sedan while his wife watched from the doorway of their house. I could see her over his shoulder, through the windshield, my legs jammed against the dashboard. All over the front lawn were children—maybe theirs—I don't know. But it stuck with me, all those eyes on me. I'd never felt so ashamed.

I tried to imagine, sometimes, when I was out there with them. I wanted to feel the way my husband had, like these wonderful animals wanted something from me. That they thought about sex as pleasure in the same way. When I was a child, I'd once come into the barn and seen a young stallion rocking so that his penis slapped his stomach. I'd run right out of there, but drew it in my diary later. But we didn't have stallions anymore, only geldings and mares. The only virile males around were the farmhands, not any of the horses. But still. I thought about it as I ran too. My husband. The dog. Horses. Sex and hair and why it was normal to have me want to fuck him but not normal for me to want to be fucked by anyone outside the marriage and not normal for him to want to fuck...well...it.

He didn't call me. I'd expected him to. Not that I was ever going back. But we'd been friends, hadn't we? I thought that was what all those years had really been about.

I worked with Lisa in the kitchen, chopping an onion. It'd always made her cry, ever since she was a girl. I guess it's normal to cry while chopping onions, but I'd never had a hard time with it. I blamed my long lashes, but Lisa laughed when I said that. "Oh, Penny, that's just another one of those things you make up," she said.

"Things I make up? What do you mean?"

"Come on," she said, "you know exactly what I'm talking about."

I was furious and chopped the onion and then held the cutting board up to her face. "Sniff deeply," I said.

She shoved me, and pieces of onion spilled onto the floor. I kicked them underneath the counter instead of bending down, and she fished them out with a broom, scooped them into the dustpan, and threw them away. "Such a nuisance," she said.

It lay by our feet, but I was too tired from work that day to say anything about it. We'd had a new horse show up for boarding, and she'd been harder to handle than the others. She had a hard time trusting. A big grey beauty. There was something pure about the way she resisted going into the stall she'd share with two others. I told Lisa all about her.

"I haven't seen you this happy in a long time," she said.

"I'm not happy," I said. "I'm fucking miserable."

We stuffed the chicken together, Lisa holding its legs open for my hand.

That night I dreamed again of horses. Six stood side by side. Their chestnut hair, the one grey. Manes tangled together. I worked my fingers into their coats, I rubbed until dust blew up. Then I was on the back of the grey one. I wasn't wearing any clothes, just my skin against the hair, my breasts pressing against the horse's mane. The horse was running and I was hanging on. I would hold on as long as I needed to.

The first thing I thought about in the morning was the woman in the sedan. I ran to the subdivisions and tried to remember which house was hers. Two houses had For Sale signs in front of them. Maybe she was leaving forever. Maybe I'd never see her again, would never be able to give her the speech I had planned about not being such an idiot and falsely accusing someone.

The run home brought the dream back to my mind and it was as if all that stupid anger about the bitch in the sedan had been removed from my forehead like a picked hoof. I couldn't wait to see my grey.

It was waiting in front of the barn, chewing on a bone it must have gotten from Lisa. They call that breed a chocolate lab, but its fur was more like the chestnut of the horses, a rust. I called him by his name and walked past him into my barn.

SO RAW
YOU CAN'T SIT

Maybe to die is like an orgasm. Being swallowed up by something you can't see coming. Yanking you from your own existence. Could it also come with pleasure? A release? "Robert, put the kettle on," I say. "Please."

"Is it your shoulder?" he asks me.

I close my eyes. "Please."

The kind of work you do when you're young, it wrecks you forever. Everyone expects you to work and live a life without pleasure. My parents included. They loved each other, I could tell, but even now, I still doubt my father knew how to make my mother come. Life was only about work, raising a family, which is work too.

I was a telephone operator. Worked in phone sales and then call centres once operators were outmoded. Now left with a shoulder that can barely move, hearing that isn't there. A ping that still rings in my right ear in the middle of the night, letting me know a call is coming in, but when I wake up, there's only dark, only Robert's uneven breaths. Feeling the safe heat of him next to me, running a hand over his skin, half-translucent like parchment paper.

Why didn't anyone tell me that you can ask a man to lick you, suck you, why didn't anyone even tell me about the clitoris, why didn't I find this out until I was twenty-seven and running away from a marriage I'd barely wanted in the first place? Unfair to have had those years wasted and to have found Robert only once I was seventy, my days already full of pain.

He's making tea in the kitchen. I'm smoking a joint. It makes the pain better, and the sex. And there is also another pain, the one we don't talk about, Robert and I, that I spoke about only with the first man I was truly in love with. It sits on your chest like a small man waiting with nothing sexual about him at all. He's a child, at night he curls on your breasts and pushes them down, flattens them. He whispers in your failing ears in the morning. All those good things are undeserved, he whispers, and won't matter eventually. Weed and sex, that's all that makes him quiet, lessens his weight just a little bit.

I didn't fall in love until I'd already discovered sex. A tender man with dark, curly hair whose acceptance and trust in me was everything. When I described the small man to him, at first he didn't really understand what I meant. He thought I was seeing things, hallucinating. I told him I was talking about feeling, and then he nodded, and he put his head on my chest. Could my husband have done that? What about the men before the man I loved? Could they have put the part of themselves with a brain on the place I was hurting and had always hurt?

I miss my first love from time to time. We had a terrible fight and parted ways. He didn't like how many men I was seeing. I didn't like that he was possessive. Couldn't it be enough that I loved him with all of myself, that his head on my chest had shooed away that little man?

Part of me wonders what it would be like to be here with him. If I'd been able to commit back then. But then there would have never been a Robert. But maybe the little man would have left for good. But it's ridiculous, playing what if.

Robert never found a place for his head on my chest, but he makes the little man quieter with our talks that begin in the morning and end at night, by stopping my brain with his movement, his body on mine.

They say love erases death, but really it is sex. And only sex. Just in the moment, and you try to get more and more until it all is gone.

Each morning, I beg Robert to put it in me raw, and he shakes his head, squirts lube on his hand, and rubs it on me, taking his time until I hold his hand there, still, rocking and moaning.

And once I never knew what lube was!

He likes my hair grown out everywhere, loves the smell of me all over, wants to make me feel whole and pure, wants to make me feel, rubs himself all over the front of me, his tip touching the most charged part of me, gently. A different type of kiss. And he puts it into me and he comes, the one time he can come each day. Then he licks me so I'll come again.

"And another?" he asks me.

"And *another*," I say, although I almost can't breathe through feeling free and numb and full of joy all at the same time.

"Do you want more?"

"More, please, more."

How many more will I have anyway? I get six, maybe eight a day, and then, and then?

And then the day floats on, I smoke some grass, I sit in my robe, the days, periods of time from one moment of being close to Robert to another. I worry sometimes, that the desire won't come back, that I'll be too old, too weary to feel our joy, but by night, he's always ready to lick, to touch me again.

Sometimes his kids call and disrupt our routine. My womb was no good for children, and after my first miscarriage with my husband, I left. And before I left, I didn't really understand sex.

Just something he did to me.

Over quickly.

After leaving, my life was mine, my breasts were mine, my pussy. My first real lover after I left my husband taught me to call it pussy, got rock hard. "Because it's soft?" I asked him coyly, wrapping my body around his bottom half and sucking the tip of him in my mouth. "Does it make you feel powerful?"

He liked being the teacher. It was about him feeling powerful, even if he denied it.

Robert comes back into the room, carrying my tea. His hip gives him trouble, but he doesn't complain as much as I do. I like to think it's because it doesn't hurt him as much, or that the pain doesn't scream, *You're old! You're old!* in the same way, in a way that makes me angry for my wasted days with my first husband, when, despite what all my lovers since have claimed, I know I was the most beautiful.

I still sometimes wonder. About that baby I didn't have, what it would have become, who.

Oh god, the pain is growing. My shoulder. My chest. Or all the pain is growing bigger than anything. Maybe this is it, how can you ever tell the difference between the little man when he's stomping so hard and your heart the moment before it gives out?

"What is it?" Robert's standing by me, I can feel him. I can always feel him, wherever he is in the house, his hand reaches for me, for my shoulder in so much pain I think it must not be attached to me anymore, nothing is attached to me, not muscle, not skin, not brain, not breasts, not pussy, only pain that throbs and twists, swells and spreads—and yes, it's like coming, the pain, because I can't even really think anymore—just Robert, just his hand pressing, trying to reattach everything, his body holding my body.

Each morning and night, the strangest things pop into my mind, as Robert pleases me, right before it goes blank with that sweet spark of life. Sometimes I think of my father, or not just my father, all of them, my mother, my sisters, each married off the way I was, but none with a shameful divorce like I had. When I went to my mother to tell her my marriage was over, she asked me, "Did he hurt you?" as if the only thing that would make her accept divorce was if he'd put his hands around my neck, almost hoping that was what I'd say, but except for when I'd told my husband I loved him, I've never been a liar, so I told her no. That we'd lost the baby and there just didn't seem to be any point.

"You work through these things," she said. "You can't expect it to be easy."

I'd wanted to say, *I don't expect it to be easy, but I expect it to be right.* But nothing ever felt right until I met Robert, and even then there were messy things, like his children not understanding how he found a love like this so late in life, even though it's been ten years now, or this one time he held me while we looked in the mirror and said we were two old souls in old bodies here ready to go through to the end together, and then that little man rose up out of my chest, and he didn't just sit there, he put his little hands right up my old nose and shoved, and I was crying before I knew any better.

The little man has his hands up there now, and I try to breathe but can't. Please, I don't want to go first. Let him go first, let me stay, I'd rather live days of pain and missing than go into the black.

Why, when I'm closest before the mind goes blank and I feel Robert's tongue, do I remember closing the door to my mother's house? Remember being thrown over my father's knee and spanked for stealing something from my sisters, my bottom so raw I thought I'd never be able to sit. Remember the penis of my first lover, swollen and stiff, the tip in my mouth. Remember my love and cradling his head to me and it all floods me so hard, there are tears in my eyes, and trembling all over, and then I can't even think anymore. Not about children or Robert or my family or loves from the past—who most surely are dead, aren't they? But I still would trade anything for one more moment of this life, full and beautiful.

OLIVES

Toward the end of the last semester I taught, before I became involved in the labour movement, I went to a cocktail party with some of my colleagues. Suzanne had invited us all through email.

Subject: Cocktails!

Hi friends,
Let's get together for a little cocktail soirée! Some of us have discussed this, but here are the firm deets:

Date: Friday, Dec. 1
Location: chez moi – 76 Clinton Street, Apt 2, ring top bell
Time: 8 pm
Attire: workplace inappropriate
Conversational topics to prepare: see above
Partners welcome?: absolutely, provided they are willing to endure/participate enthusiastically in work-bashing (the theme of the night is CATHARSIS)
Pets welcome?: no, Olive will subjugate them
What to bring: alcohol

It was during my period of self-imposed celibacy. After Brad. I walked down to the party from my apartment, where I lived alone. I talked to a friend on my cell while I walked because loneliness sometimes snuck up on me. Especially in the winter. Something about the way snow fell and then piled up on the ground and then melted away. How it was such an inconvenience. Everyone else who was coming had a partner, and I was comforted by telling myself that Suzanne was also single and it would be fine to show up alone. That being alone was a choice of mine and part of a plan to make myself more content with who I was and my decisions. Because Brad, along with most of my major relationships, had been full of bad decisions.

I was the first one there, as usual. When I got upstairs, a Boston terrier rushed me, squiggling her brown-and-white body around, pawing at me. "Olive, down," Suzanne said. Her workplace inappropriate was a sexy skirt and shirt, mine was sweats. It occurred to me that maybe I was depressed, but soon Olive had me laughing and squealing. Olive kept trying to push her pig's-knuckle bone into my mouth. "She wants to feed you."

"My grandmother's name was Olive," I said, and then told the dog a family joke featuring her name. Suzanne laughed because Olive couldn't.

I fed myself. I shoved olives into my mouth and bread with goat cheese and fig spread. "Fig jelly, fig jam," my colleagues said, and talked all about the jam they had at home. Olive curled up beside me and slept, her heat keeping my sweatpants warm.

Suzanne made us Quebec Sours, since she wanted to move to Quebec—we were all making escape plans to get out of teaching, or at least teaching college. Some of my colleagues thought teaching kids would be easier, that there would be more hope in it, but I'd done that in my twenties, and it was one of the many heartbreaking factors that led to my divorce from Travis, who I now wasn't sure was alive or dead.

Somehow, I had the most carefully laid plan. I'd never been like this before, although I'd always found a way to work. But I'd fallen into things rather than pursuing something, and

I was finally feeling ready to chase something that mattered to me. I'd helped negotiate a new contract for us through the union and fallen in love with that type of work. It felt good to be optimistic about something, in a way I hadn't been before.

To make our drinks, Suzanne mixed bourbon, apple juice, lemon, maple syrup, and this vegan faux egg white she had in one of those cocktail things you shake. Oh, a shaker. It's called a shaker.

She placed a perfectly sliced piece of apple in each one, handed them to us. "Now we're going to play a game," she said.

"I love games," said one of my colleagues.

"It's called Truth."

"Aw, man."

"Give me a question," I said. "Ask me anything." I'd already had so much to drink I was yelling.

"All right, Sam," Suzanne said. "What's the worst thing you've ever done?"

Whenever one of my parents called late at night, I assumed the other one had died. Logically I knew it could have been someone else in the family, but, growing up, I felt that a family couldn't be bigger than me, my mother, my father, and my little sister. Our parents had us when they were in their early forties, and my father told me constantly that since his mother and brother had died before they reached sixty, he doubted he'd live to see our teen years. But he did. And I think he was maybe surprised by what he saw, or surprised to find himself still living as he approached sixty-five and then seventy. I, personally, had thought I might commit suicide before I got out of my early twenties and then made myself a deal to keep going for a few more years. If I'm being truthful, I'd thought I'd never live to see my thirties, but while with Brad, I told myself I had to make one good decision for every bad one, and many of those led me in the direction of life, how about that. I'm sure that's how my dad felt too.

So when my mom called me as I was leaving the cocktail party, drunk, I thought she'd be calling to tell me my father was dead. But no. He was only in the hospital.

***

"You're not going to want me, Sam," Brad had said. "I'm disappointing. I don't do the dishes, I can be mean, I get frustrated easily, sometimes I want to be alone, sometimes I do stupid things, I'm an idiot, really."

***

When I woke in the morning, I planned on calling my sister. I had told my mom I'd tell her. But instead I went to the mirror. I knew something was wrong. Just under my eyebrows and scattered at the corners of my eyes, along the lids, were pin-prick bruises—petechiae. It looked as if I'd been punched. But really it was because I had drunk too much and had a blood disorder, thin blood. In some circles on the internet, people believed stress caused it to flare up.

And I knew breaking up with Brad, my father in the hospital, and the bruises along my eyes seemed unrelated, that everything should be unrelated. But all taken together, they made me feel like a loser. And I also profoundly missed Brad, wished I could call him instead of my sister. And then I was so angry at him because I couldn't call him and then was so angry with myself for getting involved with him in the first place. Then I felt like more of a loser.

My sister immediately put on her coat when I called and started to get her children ready to visit our parents. I could hear her barking orders, saying things about coats and snacks and telling her oldest, Michael, to help the youngest find a hat. "Are you coming?" she asked.

"How am I supposed to get all the way out there? And it's the end of the semester."

"Right, I just forgot."

"Sure, you just forgot."

"Please don't be annoyed," she said, and I could hear her voice getting all twisted up like when she wanted to cry but couldn't cry in front of her kids.

"I'm sorry," I said. "It's just stressful. And I don't like being stuck."

"I know, I know. Maybe I can drive you out from the city next weekend. If you want."

"Maybe."

"You haven't heard from Brad, have you?"

"No, why would I?"

"Just checking…"

"There's a text from him, here and there. But I try not to feed into it."

"I'm proud of you. I know how hard it is for you."

"Okay, okay."

"I love you, sister."

"Okay, okay. Text me to let me know how Dad is. And what time I should call."

***

Brad taught me to eat olives. We sat across from each other at Defina Pizza, and the olives were warm and came in two colours. He told me, "You just pop them in your mouth and bite around the pit. It doesn't have to be neat. The pit can have some stuff on it when you take it out.

I put a large dark olive in my mouth and tongued around

the pit. When I placed it on my napkin, it still had little pieces of the meat stuck to it. I call it meat because I don't know what else to call it. Flesh. The flesh.

"Here," he said, pushing a side dish toward me.

"For the pits?"

"Yeah. Try a green one. I like the green ones best."

We'd already had sex twice, and we went back to my apartment and had sex two more times. Sometimes we held hands during. He liked to look in my eyes, even though he told me later he'd never had a thing for eyes, never paid attention to them really. I told him, "I'm obsessed with hands. You've beautiful hands."

Later he told me that honesty was one of the most important things to him. I wondered if this was because he struggled with it himself. He picked me up, and I wrapped my legs around him, my face pressing into his shoulder. The fabric of his shirt was soft and he had shown me where the collar was ripping and said, "It used to be such a nice shirt." He dropped me on the bed, and then I had to laugh, the way we were together, rolling and kissing. It always reminded me of otters, how they swim around and around each other when they are playing. Or how they sleep, floating on the water, clasping hands.

We decided the affair was over. "On hold," he said. He told me the word *affair* made him feel old. But you could call it little else when two adults were doing what we were doing. We stood in my shower and discussed the parameters of the break. It was January, and my bathroom was cold. He crossed his arms in front of himself inside the damp heat of the shower before stepping into the water. "I always cross my arms like this in the shower," he said. "Like I'm going back into the womb."

I crossed my arms over my breasts. "Me too." The water beat down on us, although he was mostly standing in it, and

I was standing watching him, as he pointed his face upward, eyes closed.

We agreed the break would be in a month. We wouldn't see each other during that time, although we'd still text. "We'll still talk all the time," he said. "It won't be so bad." Half of me worried that this meant he only wanted to be my friend, but when he wanted to have sex, the other half feared being used. But we'd always talked about our relationship as something else entirely. Like exploration. Like therapy. We'd set a deadline, and then the deadline was over and we met to talk and had sex four or five times that night, and then we set another break, this one with no talking for two weeks. Then the break was over, and we met again, and that had to be that.

"It's not like I'm totally cutting you out of my life," I said on the phone. I was walking back and forth in front of a McDonald's close to the college I taught at in North York. The building offered some shelter from late February's wind. "We're just taking a step back. A few steps back. So you can figure out what will make you happy."

And I wasn't sure if he was crying on the phone; we'd cried together the night before. It'd taken us three days to really come to this decision. His voice was very quiet. "I think you're right. But I'm not happy about it. It's not what I want. I wish we could still talk every day."

"We'll keep tabs on each other. It's just a few steps back. And I'm not in one of those periods…where I'm, you know, in the market for a boyfriend or anything. That's not what this was about. You were special, and I felt very strongly for you, and that's why I wanted a relationship with you. Would still want to be in a relationship with you."

I watched a seagull peck at garbage caught in a grocery bag. "I've relied on you a lot," I said. And he said he'd relied on me and that there was so much more he wanted to say but couldn't, and then we were both so sad, and it was just another breakup really, he was another one of those guys who looked at me and wasn't sure, but it all felt different. Still like the otters.

I caught myself from saying something that would make it all harder. So we said goodbye, and we hung up.

The 195 bus pulled up full of people, ready to take me to the subway and then home. I balanced as best I could, one hand holding on to a loop above my head, one hand on my phone, which I kept expecting to light up with a text from Brad, telling me it wasn't over, that he'd find a way to make it work.

Heartache never stays in the heart. It grows in you and spreads underneath every inch of your skin. It sneaks out of your mouth. Heartache can live on any surface. It follows you as you walk around the city. Heartache is something you can never remove, you can only scrape at it with your teeth. It's the hard centre of everything. Pit. The pits.

There were certain things I did that helped. I read an article that suggested taking a couple of painkillers, then going to bed. When I woke in the morning and felt that squeeze that took over my chest, I lay on my stomach. I cuddled with my cat. I went for walks in the cold. I bought myself one Americano a day. I did a little too much work every day so I was constantly distracted, so I was constantly tired.

One of my exes had gone through all the books and leaflets I had stacked on my bedside table. When he'd discovered a small photo album, he'd flipped through photos of my family, especially of my parents when they'd been just a bit older than me. He'd stared at a photo of my father for a long time. In that photo, he was handsome and intense, and you could just tell he'd been trouble. "Daddy issues," the guy had said, and put the album back and stopped taking my calls soon after.

Brad had enjoyed looking through the album, "getting to

know your folks." He didn't say anything about Daddy issues then or ever, but he thought everyone had some sort of baggage brought on by the way they'd been raised, and they had to figure out how to reconcile it with what they wanted from life.

Although I didn't realize it until I looked at the album long after Brad and I had stopped talking, he looked a lot like my father before he'd met my mother. A wide forehead; black, wavy hair; a beard so thick you could get a whole fistful if you reached for it like a newborn baby. The only thing different was the eyes, but even those had a similar distance when they met mine. My father's eyes were so dark they seemed black, but Brad didn't even know the colour of his eyes. He said they were grey or green or brown. I told him, "That's what hazel is. You didn't know that? You have hazel eyes. Eyes that change colour." And those eyes and those hands were still in my head no matter how much work I did.

Here's where the story deviates from the true course, from fragmented memory, from the eyes I couldn't forget. From the pits, the seagull pecking a grocery bag, walks in the cold. After a while without him, for one brief moment in early March, I became nothing but heartache. I was no longer embodied. I spread across streets of the chilly city, and I found myself strongest at his apartment building, and I spread all the way up, story after story, and found Brad crying with his girlfriend, and they were holding each other, and they told each other they loved each other. And they had a dog, a dog I'd never met but now was seeing, and this dog was lying near their feet as they embraced, not making a sound. As if, like me, he was waiting. And then I was gone, for one trembling minute I was part of every couple breaking up and betraying each other and reuniting. I returned to my body, and then it was just a normal day. The sun was out. I thought maybe the sun would melt some snow. Today didn't feel like a day that I would cry. I didn't know what their embrace had meant, whether they were parting or fighting or loving or all three, and I closed my eyes and tried to remember the feeling of all those people, all the heartaches around the world.

It was the second time I'd felt out of body. The first time I'd met a man in a bar and decided I liked him because he reminded me of Travis, who I never heard anything about anymore and couldn't find online despite having been legally tied together for a few years. The man left the bar because he was sweating and he thought my friends were making fun of him. He waited for me in front of this restaurant he owned, in the alcove. He lived above it. Rather than take a cab, I thought I'd walk down the street to see if I could find him. He'd changed his clothes and was smoking, waiting. He invited me in to see the bar, apologizing for leaving, explaining he'd felt embarrassed because my friends had laughed at him. I was charmed by his insecurity. I was tender with other people's insecurities, careful of them, but I think they also allowed me a reckless sense of power. As if I were indestructible because I wasn't insecure in the same way. Which was ridiculous, since insecure people are the ones who most want to destroy other people. We kissed and I watched him make me a drink. I got to ask him to make it specifically the way I liked, and then he brought his laptop over and we listened to Kanye West, and then he went to make me another drink, but I didn't go with him, instead I scrolled through the songs in his iTunes, and then I sat on his lap and kissed his neck and I sipped my drink and then—

There are bits you remember. Watching yourself as though it's a movie or a dream. Taking off your clothes voluntarily but saying you don't want to have sex. And then being in bed for a moment. Blackness and a television screen in the dark. Then nothing. Then being in the hallway, out of body, not knowing who or what you are and then needing to run away and get away because something dangerous was happening. And then realizing the nakedness and that I was an I and I was human, and I still didn't know my name, but I went up to the top of the stairs, where I begged for help through a door, avoiding the door from which I'd come, panicked that he would come back for me. A woman let me in and gave me clothes and soon my sister came to get me and later she spoke to the woman on the phone, and we all agreed to tell the cops, that it wasn't drunkenness, it had been something else.

The first time we talked on the phone instead of just texting, around Christmas several years ago, Brad told me, "I think about that story a lot. It disturbs me." He asked me what I thought had happened, if I was sure I wasn't raped. And I said I didn't know. Other people had also asked me this, more than once, but they asked in a way that made it seem like they thought I was lying. But Brad was angry and he was also scared and he wanted to understand. He said, "I feel very protective of you." When he said that, his voice, which was normally loud and sure of itself, caught in him and became slow and low and steady. He used that voice with me whenever he was being really serious, whenever he wanted to make sure I'd hang on to what he had to say.

Brad also felt I needed to learn to let go of my trauma. That I needed to let go of the idea that these things, with Travis, or the man in the bar, that they put me in this position of powerlessness, of victimhood. He said I needed to find another way to process it.

And I respected that being powerless didn't sit right with him the same way someone attacking me didn't sit right with him. Part of me felt as if he wanted to just make it all go away. And in a lot of ways, he did.

I think it's rare that someone looks at you with their grey, their green, their hazel eyes, and sees the strong parts and weak parts of you at once and likes all of them. Once, when I was upset about something he said, he told me, "I'm sorry, Sam, sometimes I forget. I know you have that really fragile side to you. But it's easy to get caught in the moment and forget." But the thing is, most people didn't see that side at all. Or chose to ignore it.

Of course, the affair wasn't over. "Do you understand me?" he said through the phone. He was drunk and I was in my friend, Steph's, study talking to him. I'd answered the phone in front of her, and this made him nervous because he was always worried about who knew, who was aware of these parts of him only I was supposed to know about. So I sat in the study while she did the dishes, the way you could only do with old friends, leaving them to clean up your mess while you made another.

"I think so," I said. "Mostly."

"Mostly." Steph had a Lamb Chop puppet that had been on the chair, and I put it face down on the computer keyboard. The puppet offered its ass to the sky.

"I do. As much as I can. In a way that surprises me."

"That's what makes it so much harder, Sam."

I promised I'd text him when I got home, and we texted late into the night, even though I had a meeting the next morning. He'd asked me if I could just be patient for a bit, and I told him I thought I had. And he'd never asked me to wait before, even though that was what I'd been doing, and I told him we'd keep things the same and I'd email him, but yes, I'd be patient.

We started emailing then, these sprawling emails that took up a page or more. I walked through the beginning of March and the fading winter looking for things to tell him. Or the world was showing me things to tell him. Brad used to show me things. He brought me magazines with stories that reminded him of the things I wrote. He'd stand in the middle of my apartment with a magazine in his hands and say, "I brought you this. I don't know,

I thought you'd like it. You know, because of the love stories. Seemed like something you would like." A man and woman were kissing on the cover. Once, he'd bought headphones on the way to my house so he could listen to audiobooks on transit, and I'd mentioned I didn't have any headphones. He pulled them out from his phone's socket and handed them to me. "You can have these. I have more at home."

Now I wanted to be the one to show him things. I sent him *The Crack-Up* by F. Scott Fitzgerald and he hated it. He called Fitzgerald "a dazzler." I wrote him back, *It's true, I'm always taken in by dazzlers.* And time was passing, and I was still alone and he was still not, even though I'm sure he felt that way constantly. The way the soul can only feel lonely apart from itself.

***

My sister texted me later on that day to update me on Dad. She said I didn't need to worry, and he was going to be okay. It was just his heart. They were going to put him on blood thinners. "I'll be like you," he joked on the phone. "Thin blood." I promised I would come home the next weekend.

I wanted to be a good person. This desire had begun to consume me and took over almost everything I did. I'd felt it before, but only through anxiety—anxiety always postures desires as the opposite: a fear that maybe I am a bad person underneath it all. I used to make Brad reassure me, my friends reassure me, all the time, because I just wasn't sure. I knew I had some things in me that I wished weren't there, I had done some things I felt were terrible. As I struggled to decide whether to continue dating Brad or not, at the end of our relationship, I somehow realized that being a good person took many different forms because even what we took objectively to be "good" or "evil" was based on subjective concepts. I'd never believed in objectivity in any other part of my life, so I didn't know why I was applying it here. I had to come up with my own moral code and then live by it, honour it. By honouring it, I would honour myself and a respect would grow there. It was actually so simple, I didn't know why I hadn't thought of it before.

***

When I met Brad at a party, I'd shown up with a platonic friend—although we sometimes flirted, we'd remained friends for years, and over dinner before the party, I'd told him about a guy I was seeing. I was describing my type to him; he was interested in what different people wanted, physically. My description of my ideal was Travis, before he'd started getting skinnier and meaner. But I didn't tell my friend that. I tried to avoid talking about my divorce, but those few years of my life with Travis always hung around whenever I talked to friends who'd known me back then. My new guy was that Travis-type too.

We walked up the two flights of stairs to my friend's apartment, curry still on our breaths. When we entered, Brad jumped up to shake our hands right away. He wasn't the type I'd described to my friend, but something about him broke my heart instantly. I wasn't looking especially beautiful myself, wearing a bulky blue sweater to ward off the cold, but I was full of the confidence of newly dating someone. Brad sat in between my friend and me and asked us if we were dating. I said, "Oh no, but I have a boy..." but I couldn't even look at Brad as I said it. I knew the moment I looked into his eyes, I was done for, and I was prepared to delay it as much as possible. We made stupid jokes and laughed all night. I asked my friends, "What's that guy's name?" and repeated it to myself so I wouldn't forget, even though I was thinking I was falling for the man I was dating, I was thinking Brad was just a new friend. When he put on his coat, I called out, "Where's my new BFFL going? I thought we'd be best friends forever." But he didn't say goodbye to me, he just left. My friend and I left the party soon after.

In a cab, we talked about how we'd liked meeting so many new people at the party. He said, "I wasn't sure about that Brad guy."

And I said, "I knew that guy. I grew up with guys like that. I just got him. I liked him."

It took no time at all. I pursued Brad by confronting him the next time we were out with that same group of friends, telling him he hadn't been able to get me out of his head, that he was in love with me already and that we'd get married.

He said, "Let's go run off and elope right now!"

"Actually?" I said.

He said, "You're killing me, Sam!" and slapped the table with his open palm. He asked me where I lived. I pointed across the room at the man I was supposed to be dating and said that I wouldn't do anything to hurt him, that he was a good man. But really, I had been the one unable to get Brad out of my head. He pointed across the bar too and said, "What's so great about him?" We were both being so bad together. I listed off the man's positive qualities: that I could count on him, that he'd helped me out a lot when I left Travis, that he was trustworthy, a really good person. Inside my head, a little voice wanted to add, *But I'm not like that and that's not what I want.* Brad already made me so excited. As if I could do anything, as if I was the greatest person in the world.

"You're in love with me already," I said.

"I just met you! I don't even know you."

"But you do," I said.

He looked as if I'd slapped him. "Yeah, I do."

"So what are you going to do about it?" I said. "You have

a girlfriend. I heard you're practically married. What are we going to do?"

"We'll keep talking," he said. He put his head into his hand and looked me in the eyes. "We'll get to know each other. And we'll keep talking."

In two days, I broke up with the man I was seeing and began to text Brad.

***

The family joke we had went like this. "Knock, knock," my dad would say.

"Who's there?" my sister and I would shriek.
"Olive."
"Olive who?"
"Olive you!!!!"
I love you.

***

Brad and I had resumed our affair as if no time had passed, and I spent most of my time making it easier for him to contact me and waiting. My ringer was always on and loud, in case Brad called. He called me twice a day—once on his way to work, once on his way home from work. If he was off, he'd either come to see me or he'd find a way to call me, usually on the way back from getting a drink with a friend. Sometimes he'd call me when he woke up and we'd talk for several hours or text away about sex and what we'd been reading until his girlfriend got home. With Brad, my whole life became sex: I'd started watching porn, I masturbated on a schedule, and only thought about him.

On one cool summer evening, I was walking with two bags of groceries over my shoulders when I heard my phone ring. It was him, but it was 8:00 p.m. and I usually never heard from him around that time because it was when she was home. "Are you okay?" I asked. Something had to be wrong—he sounded all different, all soft teasing gone from his voice. He told me he was fine, that he'd let me get back to walking with my groceries, he was just checking in.

I heard from Brad again in an hour. He told me he and his girlfriend had broken up. He used her name. He'd started to use her name more around me, and in this way, I'd started to get to know her. He told me for the first time that she wanted a baby, kids, wanted to get married soon and have a family, and he didn't want to have kids. He corrected himself: he didn't want to have kids with someone he couldn't imagine being with forever, but I knew that wasn't what he'd told her.

He listed off the practical details of their split. He'd already found an apartment. He'd been looking since they'd seriously started discussing breaking up, and he had already signed the lease. He'd move in two days and then they'd split custody of the dog. She'd be able to afford the apartment on her own, but he didn't know if she'd want to.

Later that week, I helped him unpack his books and kitchen stuff, folded his clothes and helped hang things up. Brad was listless, slumped across his bed for most of the time I was there. Although the bed was the same one they'd shared, it seemed as if finally things were working out the way they'd been supposed to, even if it'd taken six months more than I'd originally hoped, and even if it meant that I had a strange taste in my mouth, like rust or bile, whenever I thought about any of it. I know what that taste was now.

I told him, "I know it's hard. Someone is in your life and then they aren't."

I was talking about Travis, but also about the kids I taught while we'd lived in Northern Ontario. Teaching here in Toronto was different, with clear separation from one year's class to the next, a natural end. There, the school was so small that I knew all the kids' stories and knew that even if I helped them for one day, most of them were stuck there and would end up like their parents or like Travis, tormented by something I'd never fully understand. You ended up committing yourself for the kids who were brilliant, determined to change their community, or change themselves, no matter how hard it was.

When I looked over at Brad, he was staring at the ceiling. I had wanted to talk more about leaving Travis, how it was difficult and necessary to take a step toward enjoying who I was as a person. When I'd first left and returned to Toronto, anything seemed possible—I would be single for a while and find passion in work somehow. But I'd ended up teaching college and ended up meeting Brad, and nothing had been the way it was supposed to be.

Brad's eyes were turning red in the corners, maybe from holding back tears. "Come here," he said, and spread his arm across the part of the bed that was empty, where she used to lie. I folded myself into him. "Do you want to watch me jerk off?" he said. I nodded, and he pulled down his pyjama pants and held me against his chest while I watched his hand move faster and faster over himself. He held me so hard against his shoulder that it pressed against my cheek and the edge of my eye. I felt like when I'd been with Travis, paralyzed and not seen for who I was. And then he came.

You are foolish.
You are foolish.
You are foolish.
You are foolish.
You are foolish.
You are foolish.

You are foolish.
You are foolish.
You are foolish.
You are foolish.
You are foolish.
You are foolish.
You are foolish.
You are foolish.
You are foolish.
You are foolish.
You are foolish.
You are foolish.
You are foolish.
You are foolish.
You are foolish.
You are foolish.
You are foolish.
You are foolish.
You are foolish.
You are foolish.
You are foolish.
You are foolish.

There were nights when, after we fell asleep at his new one-bedroom apartment and his back turned to me, I'd cry, privately, comforted and terrified by the dark. Wondering about what I was involved in now. In the morning, Brad's eyes were often red and I never knew when he was upset or depressed. I always thought it was about me, and that made me self-centred. Other times, he told me how important I was to him, touched my face, kissed me all over my cheeks. Sometimes he would get closer to my mouth and I would move my face to the side—I always avoided kissing his mouth when I could. I was afraid of him, afraid of all of it, not wanting to let myself fall too hard.

***

Back when we were having the affair, when he whispered in my ear if he could put himself in my ass, I said yes. I'd only let Travis do that, and the very rareness of it was enough for me to fully let go for the first time with him. My hands clasped my bedspread, his breath was hot against my cheek, his beard rubbing against my skin. I reached up and grabbed his hair then, his thick black hair between my fingers. I just wanted to be as connected as possible. For once, I was fully present, and then it was over, his body collapsed on top of mine, panting.

After he broke up with his girlfriend, I wanted to do everything with him. We found things that neither of us had ever done, although I could never tell when Brad was lying. I would text him complicated fantasies of the two of us and then when he got home, he couldn't keep his hands off me. He rarely could keep his hands off me in general, until the end. We'd be cooking or I'd be washing dishes, and he'd come up behind me at the sink and press against me, letting me feel him hard against me. Then he'd pull my pants down right there, as I said, "Brad, my hands are wet," but not be able to stop laughing and then not be able to stop. It was so easy to turn my brain off with Brad, and my brain, which has always been buzzing, looking for answers and uncovering secrets, is my enemy.

***

On one of my trips home, my father lay on the couch and I sat across from him in the living room chair where I used to hide and read.

"Why did you cheat?" I asked him. Before we started dating for real, I had once asked Brad this question in the present tense as we lay side by side on my bed after having had sex. In the dark, I felt like I had no bones in me, once again out of body, maybe a ghost, living in the dark of the room, there to search out his words. He answered me with a question—"Why don't you?" And I tried to explain what happened to me when I fell in love, and he tried to explain to me about why what we had was special, but that it might not erase the need to be with other people. The quivering ghost-me had shrunk in the dark and floated away.

My father said, "Because I was shallow." He'd been forty when he left his ex-wife for my mother and had had affairs before. He'd never cheated on my mother—I could always tell he was telling the truth. Wanted to feel he was telling the truth. "I wanted to feel loved. I wanted to feel like I could make someone feel good and that they could make me feel good."

"Did you ever feel guilty about it?" I asked.

"No. I felt terrible when I left my wife for your mother. It was painful. But I don't regret it."

I didn't know how that could be true. My sister and I had grown up knowing what he'd given up—a life of freedom—to make us. But his voice was the same as when he told the truth.

***

Shortly after Brad and I broke up, I took a road trip with a few friends to a cottage. We needed a break from work. One of my friends was considering initiating a similar affair, so I told her, "I regret it every day. I think about her all the time, how she must've felt, if she knew. If she ever knew with the other ones. And then I look at my parents—it's a life of pain. It's starting with guilt and agony. No one wants that. You want the start of a relationship to be happy, not painful. It should be full of joy." Soft singing came from the back seat, covering my words. My friend continued to sing along to the radio, looking out the window, and I pulled my knitting out of my purse, silent, and began to knit.

***

Brad and I talked about trying to escape our family patterns when we first met. I feared becoming my parents—or maybe just feared becoming an amalgamation of their negative traits, which I was certain I was. I was fussy at times, could be brooding, could be too overbearing one second and then too distant the next, and I was dissatisfied with life.

One of the first things we did when we began to text, before the issue of sex or anything like that came up, was tell each other our life stories. I was, as my father had raised me to be, fully honest, giving him the details of my heartbreaks and Travis and what it felt like to be terrified of someone you loved, to watch them change and deteriorate into someone you couldn't be around. In several connected text messages, I told him about my parents and how they got together, that it'd been an affair and they still really loved each other, you could tell, but that their relationship seemed unbalanced to me and I feared I was drawn to something like that. I wanted a healthy relationship more than anything.

Brad felt similarly about his family, yet at first seemed to have very little baggage left over from them or anything. He mentioned a series of girls, none of whom had meant too much, rather than talking about his girlfriend. As I got to know Brad more, I discovered much of what he said in the beginning had been a lie. I didn't understand why someone would want to lie or conceal parts of themselves. It didn't make sense to me. I always wanted to know everything and tell everything—figure out who did what and when—until I could make linear sense of everything and, growing up, none of my parents' answers were ever detailed enough for me.

Brad was an accountant, but I liked to tell him he had the soul of a poet, which always caused him to scoop me up and dump me on the bed. But it was true, and it was perfect, no matter how teasing and lame my description. He was always something that appeared to be something else.

**

My sister picked me up the next weekend, and instead of Brad, we talked about my father and our family the whole time, how it was that the two of us had come to be. "Have you ever thought about having an affair?" I asked her. "Even just a little bit?"

"Of course," she said quietly, checking the rear-view mirror to make sure her sons were asleep. "But it's just not practical, so I'd never do it."

Practical. So typical of her. "But isn't there love? A moral block?"

"I'm not sure. I mean, I love Danny, of course, but there's still attraction that you feel sometimes and you wonder about certain situations. Like it changes, right? I mean, like, what if he was sick? What if he cheated? What if we were apart for a really long time because of work?"

"But isn't it wrong?"

She looked at me then, not watching the road, her windshield wipers whisking the snow from the glass. And in an instant, she was our mother, like if she wanted, she'd be able to punch me with her eyes. "Well, you did it, didn't you?"

I was silent then.

She changed the conversation to discussions of the future.

Most people don't really recognize the worst thing they've ever done. They have bad times, periods of time when they felt they became a little lost. They were young. They didn't know what they were doing. But this is because the worst thing they have ever done is an accumulation of all the little bad decisions. These decisions don't feel morally wrong in the moment, they feel like something outside of yourself. Maybe, if you believe in fate, even destined. After Brad, I came to feel that I only believed in fate and destiny as a game, because I knew that, in every moment, I had had the chance to make a different decision, that I still had free will, I'd just chosen to pretend.

And this was why I cried in the dark beside him. When I closed my eyes at night, I saw her, his girlfriend. I thought of her name. Was it just because I was in her place now? Brad and I were planning to move in together, but there were these occasional patches of time when I was unable to reach him—of course, always paired with a later excuse that made me feel that it was possible—no, probable—that he still had someone else on the side. And all the little ways he withheld. But no, this isn't about that, it's not about all his small betrayals and his lies. It's not about all the things that led to us not seeing each other anymore. That's the problem, that I always saw it being about Brad.

While I was being taught how to eat olives, she was maybe at home, bored, watching TV on a couch they shared. Or she was out walking their dog, cutting through February's wind. As we debated the details of our affair while the shower threw water down on us, discussed whether our situation could continue, maybe she was talking on the phone with one of her friends. Maybe she was worrying about where he was or wondering when he would come back. More likely, she thought he was somewhere other than where he really was, and this disturbed me. I thought about how she had a picture in her mind of where her partner was that didn't match where he actually was—in my bed, kissing me, trying to look me in the eyes. That maybe she was washing the dishes as he held me as I cried, asking him why we couldn't be together, and maybe she was putting away the dishes as he whispered to me, "Let's make love."

Once we reached the country, we pulled my nephews from their car seats and set them down, and they ran inside to see their grandpa. I shyly hung back, offering my hands to grab whatever she wanted to hand me. "I'm sorry," she finally said, "for what I said in the car."

"It's fine," I said, and it was. I was the one who had done it in the first place. Now the rest of my life would be about living with it.

I wondered if it was like that for our parents. For my father, who spoke openly about the pain of his divorce. For my mother, who had been in the same position as me, so convinced that love would make things work. Had it made them angry the way it'd made me angry—to realize that you took a gamble and risked it all for something that only looked like love on the surface and then were stuck with disappointment? I thought of my mother setting the table, she and my father always in each other's way in the kitchen. They were both angry, but maybe that was the type of little anger that the daily tedium of life brought and that Brad's and my real failure was not being able to deal with it.

In the morning, we all took a walk except my mother. She preferred to stay at home when it was cold, curled up with a book. I knew she liked her moments of quiet. My dad took a long walk every day, no matter the weather, as a means to keep his blood sugar low. I took my youngest nephew, who was named Daniel, after his father. I called him Danny the Second. My sister held Michael's hand. Danny the Second said, "Sam, snaps," to me before we went out, and I snapped his jacket shut for him, one snap at a time from the bottom, and then flicked his nose, and he beamed at me, pushing open the screen door and running after his mom, his brother, his grandfather. He walked two steps into the snow, up to his knees, and then stopped. "Sam! Up!" he said, and so I scooped him up into my arms, his boots banging against my stomach, dampening my down jacket as the snow stuck to them melted.

"Sam," my sister called back. She had slung the boys' skates, knotted at the tips of their laces, around her neck. We were going to teach Danny the Second to skate for the first time. "Don't carry him, he can do it. We just got out here."

"It's just so deep," I said, and Danny the Second tightened his grip on my shoulders, as if he needed me.

"If we coddle him, he'll turn out like all the guys you've dated," she said, and Danny the Second, not knowing what that meant, squiggled his release from my arms and hopped through the snow until he rejoined his brother.

My dad waited for me, and my sister ventured forward, guiding her sons toward the path that would lead us to the lake. My parents had grown up beside the Cross-Canada Trailway, and that was where he liked to take his walk, quietly appreciating the place where he'd always lived. When I caught up with him, he slipped his hand into mine, glove on glove. As a child, sometimes I'd made him take off his glove on the hand that held mine. He would hold my hand and slip his glove or mitt over both of our hands, thinking I needed to be kept warm. But really it had just been because I wanted to feel the heat of his skin. His skin was almost nothing now, bones showing through. He used to talk to me about death, as if a whole universe could open up from his confusion and despair about a world that would end. Or not that the world would end, but that he would, who he was, his consciousness. But as he got older, he voiced those thoughts more rarely.

We got to the lake, and my father and I stood at the top of the hill, while we watched Michael and Danny the Second cut down ahead of their mother, through snow-covered reeds, adventurers. I studied my sister watching her sons, wary and prepared for whatever happened. Maybe one day it would be possible for me to have a family. I had that steadiness about me. I was dedicated to changing my life, not falling into the same traps, and I'd found that passion I'd been looking for, a new career, how about that. I just had to be wary of feelings. Feelings that changed, the way unfrozen lake water in different light changes from brown to green to grey.

*Sometimes when you peek in,
someone is staring back.*

ACKNOWLEDGEMENTS

I would like to thank all the people who came together to make the last year of my life a little easier—It's amazing to me that a little book like this is flying free after such a difficult time and year.

Craig Calhoun, thank you for your support during these final stages of putting the book out and for your love and support of everything I am and do. I am so grateful that you exist in this world and have become a part of mine.

Sofia Mostaghimi, let's hang out on a roof and look out over the city. Let's dance all night long. Thank you for continuing to be my bffl, for your edits, for writing work the world needs to see.

Michelle, you are part of my family. Vincent, so are you. Bo, please be my new baby and move in. M & V, I am so impressed by your vibrancy every day and the way you both create!

So much love to all of my friends who visited me in the hospital, championed my writing, or were just a listening ear. I am nothing without all of you.

To past editors of these pervy stories, whether formally or informally: Catriona Wright; Joe Thomson; Andrew Battershill; Nadia Ragbar; Cheryl Runke; Menaka Ramen-Wilms; Corina Milic and Brett Popplewell at *The Feather Tale Review*; Conan Tobias at *Taddle Creek*; and Anita Chong, Sharon Bala, Kerry Clare, and Zoey Leigh Peterson for putting the *Journey Prize 30 Anthology* together. Thank you for seeing something in these stories and making them better.

Thank you to everyone who worked on this book: my agent,

Marilyn Biderman, for believing in new writers and getting our work out into the world; Meg Storey for her wonderful editing and her vision for *Just Pervs*; Tree Abraham for the powerful cover design that captures *Just Pervs'* galloping spirit; Stuart Ross for his keen copy edits; and Hazel, Jay Millar and the rest of the Book*hug team for all of their hard work putting out excellent books.

Shout out to my colleagues at CUPE 3902: keep making a difference! Thank you for making me a better person.

And thank you so much to my family, especially Mom, Dad, Kenny, Beata, and Lukas. Thank you for always supporting my creative projects, even the gross ones.

Stories from *Just Pervs* were previously published in *Taddle Creek*, *The Feathertale Review*, *This Magazine*, and *The Journey Prize Anthology 30*. The title story, "Just Pervs" appeared in a chapbook of the same name by Desert Pets Press.

I am grateful to the Ontario Arts Council for its financial assistance during the writing process, and for its Writers' Reserve Program. Thank you to the publishers who recommended me.

"So Raw You Can't Sit" was inspired by "Extreme Sexuality in an 80-Year Old Woman" from *Extreme Sexuality in Women* by G.D. Masters.

"I Moved Out when I Caught Him with the Dog" was inspired by a news story that broke in 2015, featured in *The Daily Dot* and *Metro News UK*.

The Little Perv stories/interruptions throughout the text were inspired by "The Voyeur's Hotel" by Gay Talese in *The New Yorker*.

© Cornelius Quiring

JESS TAYLOR is a Toronto writer and poet. She founded The Emerging Writers Reading Series in 2012. *Pauls*, her first collection of stories, was published by Book*hug Press in 2015. The title story from the collection, "Paul," received the 2013 Gold Fiction National Magazine Award. Jess is currently at work on a novel and continuation of her life poem, "Never Stop." She lives in Toronto.

COLOPHON

Manufactured as the first edition of *Just Pervs*
in the fall of 2019 by Book*hug Press.

Edited for the press by Meg Storey

Copy edited by Stuart Ross
Type + design by Tree Abraham

bookhugpress.ca